the Cheetah girls

It's Raining Benjamins

Deborah Gregory

SCHOLASTIC INC.

New York   Toronto   London   Auckland   Sydney
Mexico City   New Delhi   Hong Kong   Buenos Aires

For my peeps John Moore
Whom I do adore
'Cuz he works the floor
Like a mad matador!
Toro, toro!

Fashion credits: Photography by Charlie Pizzarello. Models: Sabrina Millen, Sonya Millen, and Brandi Stewart. On Brandi (Chanel): necklace by Agatha Paris. Raincoats by Betmar. Bandanas by Le Chien. Dresses by XOXO. Shoes and umbrellas by Nicole Miller. Stockings by Sox Trot. Hair accessories by HEAD DRESS. Hair by Julie McIntosh. Makeup by Lanier Long and Deborah Wallace. Fashion styling by Nole Marin.

Visit www.cheetahgirls.com

Text copyright © 2000 by Deborah Gregory.
All rights reserved. Published by Scholastic Inc.,
555 Broadway, New York, NY 10012,
by arrangement with Hyperion Paperbacks for Children.
Printed in the U.S.A.

ISBN 0-439-41824-0

5   6   7   8   9   10   40   10

The Cheetah Girls Credo

To earn my spots and rightful place in the world, I solemnly swear to honor and uphold the Cheetah Girls oath:

🐾 Cheetah Girls don't litter, they glitter. I will help my family, friends, and other Cheetah Girls whenever they need my love, support, or a *really* big hug.

🐾 All Cheetah Girls are created equal, but we are not alike. We come in different sizes, shapes, and colors, and hail from different cultures. I will not judge others by the color of their spots, but by their character.

🐾 A true Cheetah Girl doesn't spend more time doing her hair than her homework. Hair extensions may be career extensions, but talent and skills will pay my bills.

🐾 True Cheetah Girls *can* achieve without a weave—or a wiggle, jiggle, or a giggle. I promise to rely (mostly) on my brains, heart, and courage to reach my cheetah-licious potential!

🐾 A brave Cheetah Girl isn't afraid to admit when she's scared. I promise to get on my knees and summon the growl power of the Cheetah Girls who came before me—including my mom, grandmoms, and the Supremes—and ask them to help me be strong.

🐾 All Cheetah Girls make mistakes. I promise to admit when I'm wrong and will work to make it right. I'll also say I'm sorry, even when I don't want to.

🐾 Grown-ups are not always right, but they are bigger, older, and louder. I will treat my teachers, parents, and people of authority with respect—and expect them to do the same!

🐾 True Cheetah Girls don't run with wolves or hang with hyenas. True Cheetahs pick much better friends. I will not try to get other people's approval by acting like a copycat.

🐾 To become the Cheetah Girl that only *I* can be, I promise not to follow anyone else's dreams but my own. No matter how much I quiver, shake, shiver, and quake!

🐾 Cheetah Girls were born for adventure. I promise to learn a language other than my own and travel around the world to meet my fellow Cheetah Girls.

Chapter 1

Unless it's raining alley cats and Chihuahuas, everybody at Fashion Industries East High School hangs out in front of the school, blocking the whole sidewalk. It's a real mob scene most mornings before classes start. Sometimes *la gente*—peeps—can get kinda rowdy, too.

That's why *my* crew—Dorinda "Do' Re Mi" Rogers; Galleria "Bubbles" Garibaldi; and myself, of course, Chanel "Chuchie" Simmons—always meet *inside*, by the lockers.

Dorinda is already waiting there when I arrive, forty minutes before school starts. Most of us at Fashion Industries East—which is not to be confused with the *other* Fashion

Industries High, where the less *coolio* peeps go to school—come here by subway from other neighborhoods, and you have to allow for time, 'cuz the subways—well, you know how the subways can be. So if your train happens to come on time, you can get to school *real* early, *está bien?*

Dorinda is crouching with her back against a locker, happily sipping her Goofy Grape Juice. "Wazzup, *señorita?*" she yells when she sees me.

"*Nada,* that's what," I moan, swiping a sip from her pint-sized container—which I do almost every morning, and she never complains. "I wish they sold this stuff by *my* house."

"So *move,*" Do' Re Mi shoots back, shrugging her shoulders. "Hey. Where's Galleria?"

"*Yo no sé,*" I mumble. "I can't even get decent *café con leche* by my house. Not like the kind they sell near my Abuela Florita's."

"I remember her," Do' Re Mi says. "She's phat."

"She is not fat!" I say, misunderstanding.

"No, not fat—phat!" Do' corrects me, and we both crack up.

My Abuela (that's "grandma") Florita lives in "Dominican Land," better known as Washington Heights. It's kinda far *norte*—right before Manhattan turns into *El Bronx*.

"I'm going to be seeing my *abuela* on Saturday," I tell Dorinda. "It's Pucci's birthday."

My little brother's birthday is a very big deal around my house—mostly because it means our dad comes home to visit. I can't help being excited to see him, and neither can Pucci. He doesn't visit much, not since he left home for good five years ago.

See, he and Mom used to fight all the time—to the point where they needed a referee. They're both happier now. Mom's got her rich boyfriend, Mr. Tycoon, who lives in Paris, France.

And Dad's got his new girlfriend, Princess Pamela, who is *la dopa*, and like a second mother to me. She runs Princess Pamela's Psychic Parlor, right around the corner from my house. I go see her there, whenever I can get away without Mom knowing. Sometimes, I even see Dad there. And once in a while, I visit them at their apartment uptown. But it's *different* when Dad comes *home*. And with Abuela coming, too, it'll almost feel like we're a whole family again.

Anyway, Dad says he's gonna drive up to Abuela's early Saturday, and bring her with him to the party. Abuela doesn't take the subway by herself anymore. See, last year a guy tried to snatch her purse on the subway platform. Abuela reached in her purse for the can of mace she carries, but she spritzed the mugger with her bottle of *Santa Cría* cologne by mistake! *Gracias gooseness*, the mugger ran away anyway—probably because Abuela sounds really scary when she's cursing in Spanish!

"How old is Pucci gonna be?" Dorinda asks.

"Ten—and an even bigger pain in the poot-butt," I groan—looking straight at Kadeesha Ruffin, who has just walked up to a nearby locker and slammed it shut for no reason. Then, on top of it, she gives me a look like I'm a *hologramma*—you know, a ghost—before continuing on her way down the hall.

"She thinks she's cute. *Qué bobada*. What baloney," I mumble.

"She's just green with Gucci envy," Dorinda says, still sipping, and unfazed by the intrusion.

4

"Yeah, the Jolly Green Giant," I moan. Kadeesha is kinda tall—over six feet. I'm not about to start messing with her. But why's she got to mess with *me*? What did I ever do to her, *está bien*?

Most of *la gente* at Fashion Industries East are kinda cool, because they're into a lot of different things, and they even have jobs after school. My crew's claim to fame is that everybody knows we're part of a singing group—the Cheetah Girls—who are headed to the top. There are five of us—me, Do', Bubbles, and the fabulous Walker twins—Aquanette and Anginette—who were born and raised in Houston, Texas, and go to school uptown, at LaGuardia Performing Arts High.

Lately, *la gente* have been taking notice of our *adobo down* style—especially since the Cheetah Girls got flown out to Los Angeles to perform at Def Duck Records' New Talent Showcase! I still can't believe Def Duck *paid* for us to go to the City of Angels, where record company executives drive in limousines on the big, fat freeway of deals.

To tell you the truth, I was also happy to get *away* from my mom and my brother, Pucci, for a few days. They were both driving me crazy, more than usual. That week, I would have followed the Cheetah Girls anywhere, even right into the lion's den. Well, almost.

Anyway, ever since we got back, the whole school's been buzzing about us. A few people, especially Kadeesha, have shown definite signs of Cheetah envy!

Everyone wants to know if we got a record deal. It's frustrating to have to tell them we don't know yet. But it's the truth. The peeps at Def Duck said it might be a while before we heard anything. And it already seems like a *long* while, even though it's only been a few days.

"It's gonna be *tan coolio*—so cool—wearing our new Cheetah Girls chokers together," Dorinda says, ignoring Kadeesha. "That is, unless someone tries to put a leash on us!"

This whole Cheetah Girl choker thing happened faster than making Minute Rice. See, while we were out in L.A., Bubbles bought a cheetah-print suede collar for her dog, Toto. He is so cute—I wish I could have a little dog, too. But I guess I'm never gonna have one. Not if my mom has anything to say about it—which she does. She's allergic to dog hair, and even more allergic to getting dog hair off the couch and cleaning up puppy poo.

Anyway, the collar Bubbles bought Toto was *la dopa*, but it was way too big for him. So Bubbles gets the great idea to wear it herself! That's Galleria for you—when she gets an idea, she doesn't ask anybody's opinion, she just goes for it!

Bubbles wore it to school the next day, and some of the peeps here ate it up like puppies! Five or six people asked her where they could get one. That gave Galleria *another* idea—that the Cheetah Girls should make some money while we're waiting for Def Duck to call!

Well, why not? We all need duckets—especially me. I still owe my mom plenty from the time I maxed out her charge card. (What can I say? I'm a recovering shopaholic that already happened!)

Anyway, making and selling Cheetah chokers seemed like a good idea to the rest of us. We've had a couple of orders already—and we needed to make ourselves chokers, too, so we could be walking advertisements.

We went to the factory in Brooklyn where

Bubbles's dad makes all the clothes for her mom's boutique, Toto in New York . . . Fun in Diva Sizes. Bubbles's mom and dad are my godparents—my *madrino* and *madrina*—and there's nothing they won't do to help us Cheetah Girls. *Madrina*—Ms. Dorothea, as the twins call her—is even our manager!

Anyway, we made some Cheetah Girls chokers out of suede strips, then glued silver metal letters on them that say GROWL POWER, to represent our kinda flava. So now we have these *adobo down* chokers. That is, Bubbles has them. But where is she? Homeroom starts in fifteen minutes, and we've got to find our customers before that!

As you can probably tell, I'm kinda anxious about these chokers. See, two students—Derek Hambone and LaRonda Jones—have already put in orders, and we've got to deliver them first thing today, *está bien?* I mean, I'm counting on this money so I can pay back my mom and be free again!

"There's Galleria," mumbles Dorinda, catching sight of Bubbles's head of wild-and-woolly hair coming our way.

"Finally!" I say, relieved.

Galleria is so *occupada*, writing in that notebook of hers, that she almost walks smack into a guy in the hallway! Ever since seventh grade, Bubbles has been writing in her Kitty Kat notebooks. She keeps them stashed in her bedroom, the way Pucci stashes Whacky Babies stuffed animals—like they're *muy preciosas*—very precious—in the jiggy jungle!

It's not like I don't already know Bubbles's secrets. And anyway, most of the time she's just writing another song for our group—in case we ever get to make a record. Even so, Bubbles never lets anyone see the words to a new song until *she* thinks it's finished.

That doesn't stop me, of course, from trying to snatch the spotted notebook from Bubbles any way I can. I've forgotten all about the chokers, 'cuz nothing's more *la dopa* than Bubbles's songs!

"Chuchie, lemme finish!" Bubbles screams at me, giving me a whack with her notebook. "I'm trying to come up with more songs, 'cuz I know Def Duck is gonna take a dip in the players' pond and let us cut a demo, you know what I'm saying?"

"Word. I heard that," Do' Re Mi chimes in,

brushing dust off her jumper (our school is kinda falling down all over the place, and there's plaster dust all over everything, including the lockers).

Dorinda *always* agrees with Bubbles. It annoys me sometimes—'cuz *I* know that when Bubbles and I disagree, I'm right at least half the time.

I hope Bubbles is right on this one, though. She thinks we are going to get a record deal *para seguro*—for sure—because we were *la dopa* at the showcase in Los Angeles.

I'm not so sure. Performing in a showcase and getting a record deal are two different things. But like I say, I hope I'm wrong, and I guess I must be, 'cuz Galleria's mom agrees with her, and she's almost always right! *Madrina* says all we have to do now is sit back and "wait for the bait."

Bubbles is so talented—she always gets *la dopa* ideas for songs. But lately, I've been thinking that *I* probably could write songs, too, if she would just give me a chance.

"What's the new song called—or is *that* a secret, too?" I whine, still trying to get a peek at the Kitty Kat notebook. Then I start chanting a little rhyme Bubbles made up. "Kitty Kat, Kitty Kat, show me where the money's at!"

"This song is called, 'Woof, There It Is!'" Bubbles says proudly. "And you can see it when it's done!" Then she snaps her Kitty Kat notebook shut and shoves it into her backpack, without even letting us take a peek.

"Oooh, that's a cute title!" I say.

Gloating on her skills, Bubbles gets puffed up like Rice Krispies and says, "I got the idea for the song after I showed Mom the chokers. She said they looked like dog collars—and that grown-ups wouldn't wear them!"

"Where *are* the chokers?" I ask, panicking because I don't see the Toto in New York shopping bag Bubbles put the chokers in at the factory.

"Got 'em right here in this pouch," Bubbles says, patting the tummy of her cheetah backpack. She unzips it again, and pulls out a couple of the chokers. "Wait till Derek sees his." She giggles, stretching out the leather strip to reveal the silver metal letters that spell SCEMO. (It's pronounced "shay-mo.")

"*Scemo*—that means idiot in Italian, right?" Dorinda asks. But Bubbles has already told her a million times, so she knows. See, Galleria's dad is Italian—real Italian, born in Italy!—so she knows a lot of words in that language—even the bad words.

"Don't you think Derek is gonna go off when he finds out what *scemo* means in English?" I ask. "You know what I'm saying, 'cuz he may not be playing."

"He's too big a *scemo* to find out that he *is* one!" Bubbles says, then stretches her hand out for us to do the Cheetah Girls handshake with her. I don't feel good about it, but I do it anyway.

But I don't really care about Derek Hambone. I just wanna know what *Madrina* thought of the chokers. "Was *Madrina* surprised we made them without her help?" I ask. It's not that my godmother isn't really supportive of us and the things we do—except when I ran up Mom's charge card, of course—but sometimes she does *too* much for us.

"You know she ain't saying, but I think she was really proud of us," Bubbles says.

"I heard that," Do' Re Mi says, nodding her little beanie head to her own beat.

"As a matter of facto, she looked at the

chokers and said they're off the cheetah meter, *bay-beeee!*" Bubbles screeches.

"*Madrina* thinks we can sell them?" I ask.

"Yup. Forget what Mr. Kumba-bumba-baloney said." Bubbles laughs, making fun of the name of the owner of the Kumba Boutique in Brooklyn, where we went last night to try and sell our chokers.

I guess it was a stupid idea, because Mr. Kumba thought they looked like dog collars, and that nobody would wear them. I was so glad to get out of the Kumba Boutique anyway, I remember, scrunching up my nose. "*Lo odio*— that strawberry incense he was burning— yuck!" I remind my crew.

"It smelled like a psychedelic voodoo shack or something," Dorinda remembers, laughing.

I laugh, too, and scrunch up my nose again, making a funny face like I smell something bad. That's when I really *do* smell something— and it's really, *really* stinky poo.

Bubbles says I'm prissy, but I'm not. I just don't like odors. My nose is *muy sensitiva*, and I can smell things that other people can't— just like dogs do. (I think that's why I love dogs so much—because we are a lot alike.) And *speaking of dogs* . . .

"Bubbles, do you smell doggy poo?" I ask sheepishly.

"I smell it, too . . . oh, no—don't tell me!" Bubbles looks down at her shoes, and discovers the root of the problem. "I can't believe it! I'm so *over* this!"

"Woof, there it is," Dorinda says, smirking.

I crack up, and Bubbles throws me an annoyed look. "I *hate* this city," she says. "Nobody cleans up after their dog except me, and I'm the one who winds up stepping in it!"

I try to console her by saying "We didn't see one pile of doggy poo the whole time we were in Cali."

"No, we didn't," Bubbles says wistfully. "You got that right."

"It's even worse in my neighborhood than it is here," Do' Re Mi moans. Do' lives way uptown, and her neighborhood is like *el barrio*, where Abuela lives. The people there have a lot of big, mean dogs, with ferocious fangs for protection—and just for stylin'. And those kinda dogs leave some big, stinky land mines on the sidewalk.

"I'll get it off for you, Bubbles," I volunteer. (That'll show her I'm not squeamish like she says I am.) "Come on—before anybody sees it."

"You mean, *smells* it!" Dorinda corrects me. She and I crack up, but Galleria isn't laughing. She walks on her tiptoes all the way to the bathroom, holding her nose. I walk on my tiptoes, too, like I'm wearing pointshoes—my ballet slippers.

A few people walk by, heckling at Galleria. "Sashay, parlay!" they call out, imitating her walk. Bubbles sticks her tongue out at them like she doesn't care, but I know she's goospitating inside. I know I would be—*Yo sé!*

Chapter 2

The bathroom at Fashion Industries East High is right out of a prison movie—kinda dark and creepy-looking. I make Bubbles take off her Mary Jane shoes, then throw both of them in the sink and turn on the faucet.

Nothing comes out of it. "Oh, come on," I moan. The faucets at our school are broken more than half the time. At last, a little water spurts out—then suddenly, it *gushes* out, flooding the sink, and totally soaking Galleria's shoes!

"Chuchie!" Bubbles yells, running to turn off the faucet. The water is splashing everywhere now—all over the floor, and *us.*

It's Raining Benjamins

All of a sudden, Kadeesha Ruffin flings open the bathroom door and stands there with her crew. "What's up, y'all—is it laundry day?" she asks. Her crew starts whooping it up and high-fiving each other.

I don't say anything, because Kadeesha is kinda nasty and I'm scared of her. Bubbles just ignores her while Dorinda—politely—explains the situation.

"Don't tell me y'all have never stepped in poop— So here's the scoop: back off and get out of our loop. Just leave us alone," she says. *Vaya*, go, Do' Re Mi! Her snaps are as good as Bubbles's. *Te juro.* I swear.

"Awright, shortie," Kadeesha says. She snaps her gum really loud, then marches out the bathroom without using the sink. Her crew follow behind her, still grinning, even though they're not laughing out loud anymore.

Galleria is staring at her soaked shoes, shaking her head like she's about to cry. "*Now* what do you expect me to do, Miss Cuchifrito Ballerina?" she challenges me. "Plié down the hallways all day without shoes?"

Meanwhile, I'm busy yanking brown paper towelettes from the dispenser and trying to blot her shoes dry. The truth is, I feel stupid, like a *babosa*.

Dorinda looks at the dripping shoes, and suggests hopefully, "We could put paper towels in the bottoms."

"No, *olvídate!*" I say, suddenly bursting into tears. "Just forget wearing them, okay? I'm a ding-a-ling, all right? Now just put them on the paper towels."

I can't believe I yelled at Bubbles. Suddenly I realize that it's not just the wet shoes that are bothering me. There's something else . . . something that was *annoyándome* before we went out to L.A. In all the excitement about the New Talent Showcase and the chokers, I'd forgotten all about it. Well, I *tried* to forget it, anyway, and now, that Pucci's birthday was almost here . . .

"Chuchie, what's the matter with you?" Bubbles blurts out when I can't stop crying.

"*Nada,*" I whine. Then I take out my Yves Saint Bernard perfume spray. I spritz it in her shoes, then spritz the air for good measure. "You know how I am about stinky-poos!"

"Yeah—but what's *really* wrong?" Bubbles insists, waving away the mist of my perfume (which she hates). "You're not crying over my shoes, *girlita*, so don't lie or you'll fry." It's unbelievable how Bubbles knows me inside and out!

All of a sudden, I blurt out the truth. "Saturday is Pucci's birthday, and my mom hasn't said one thing about buying him a Chihuahua like she promised!"

"Chuchie," Bubbles says, instantly putting her arm around me. "I didn't know you were so upset about that."

"You *know* how much I want a dog. I mean for Pucci," I confess. "Remember when we were at *Madrina*'s store, and my mom said she would think about getting Pucci a Chihuahua for his birthday?"

"Yeah, I remember—but I guess *she* doesn't," Bubbles says, in that tone she gets when she's trying to push me to do something. "You'd better ask her yourself."

"I don't want to," I shoot back, wiping Bubbles's shoes furiously with the paper towels. Little wet balls of paper are now decorating her shoes.

"Oh, I get it, you're *scared* to ask her, because you haven't paid back all the money you owe her," Bubbles says.

I can't wait until I pay back all the money I owe my mother for charging up her credit cards—then I'm gonna seal Bubbles's lips closed with Wacky Glue! "So?" I hiss at her. "You'd be afraid, too."

"You know it, so don't blow it," Galleria admits. She gives me a little squeeze. "I know how much you've always wanted a dog—and you *know* that little Chihuahua would be *your* dog, 'cuz no way is Pucci gonna take care of it."

"Wait a minute," Do' Re Mi steps in. "What if you offer to pay for *part* of the Chihuahua?"

"What happened? How am I gonna pay for anything?" I ask. "I got *nada* for *nada*."

We both look at Do' Re Mi like she's cuckoo, but she continues: "We're gonna sell these Cheetah Girls chokers we've made, *ri-ight*?"

"Yeah," Galleria chimes in. "But so far, we only got orders from Derek and LaRonda. One plus one makes *two*."

"Yeah, but if the *three* of us go around all week taking orders for Cheetah Girls chokers, we can get Chanel enough money so she can go to her mom and say she'll put in thirty dollars to help buy the dog for Pucci's birthday."

Do' Re Mi looks to Bubbles for approval. "I

mean, we've got all week to sell them, *ri-ight?*
And they're dope, *ri-ight?*"

Bubbles thinks hard for a minute. Then she
looks at the both of us, wild-eyed, and asks, "If
all three of us take orders, how many of these
you think we can sell?"

"I don't know—a lot, *ri-ight?*" I offer, smiling. We all give each other the Cheetah Girls
handshake, and then get busy helping Bubbles
put her wet shoes back on. I feel so much better
now that I've told Bubbles and Dorinda the
truth about what's been on my mind. They are
really my crew, *es la verdad.*

"It's our dime—and choker time," Bubbles
says, handing over Cheetah Girls chokers for
us to wear. Then she puts one on herself. The
three of us just stand there, gazing in the dirty
mirror at our cheetah-fied reflections.

"That does look so *money*, *ri-ight!*" Bubbles
says, satisfied.

"*Sí, señorita*," I say with a grin. "I can't wait
to show Abuela Florita what we're doing. I'll
bet you she'll like our chokers." I turn to
Dorinda and pinch her cheeks. "Abuela would
love you, too—because she just *loves* dimples."

"Well, it's time to turn some Cheetah Girl

chokers into duckets," Bubbles says, tickling our fingers as we do the Cheetah Girls hand-shake one more time. "Homeroom's about to jump off—we'd better get shaking if we want to sell some of these while they're still baking."

"I know what *you're* going to buy with your choker money, *mamacita*," I tease Bubbles as we leave the bathroom and start running down the hall.

"What?"

"A new pair of shoes!"

Chapter 3

Both Bubbles and I major in fashion merchandising, while Dorinda majors in fashion design. Our homeroom classes are in Building C, on the other end of the second floor. When we get there, there are still fifteen minutes till homeroom starts. We hang in the hallway till the last minute, hoping to run into Derek Ulysses Hambone—"Mr. DUH"—and give him his choker.

"Maybe Mackerel will take the bait, too," I say excitedly. "Let's hook him on a choker!"

"Just don't get caught in his trap," giggles Bubbles.

Mackerel Johnson is Derek Hambone's best friend. He has a crush on me—*un coco* that is never gonna happen, because he doesn't know that I'm going to meet *Krusher*.

Krusher, in case you live on Mars and have never heard of him, is a *tan coolio* singer, with the brain, heart, and courage to live his wildest dreams in the jiggy jungle. It doesn't matter that *I* didn't win the 900-KRUSHER contest, which would have taken me on a trip to Miami for a date with my favorite *papi chulo*—I'll find another way to meet him, you just wait and see!

"If Mackerel didn't bounce around like a jumping bean, would you go out with him?" Bubbles asks, smirking at me. She doesn't believe that my heart belongs to Krusher, but I won't settle for less, *está bien?*

"Oh, word, I've got a dope idea," Dorinda suddenly says, then whips out a book from her cheetah backpack and hands it to me. "Check this out, Chanel," she says, her eyes twinkling. "I can't believe I didn't think of this when we were talking about it before!"

"What is it, Do'?" I ask, curious.

"I've been reading about these African pygmy hedgehogs," she says.

I flip through the book, and I can't believe what I'm seeing. These pygmy creatures look sooo cute—brownish and small, with sticky spiny things on their backs. "*Qué monos!*" I coo.

"See, I was thinking maybe you could get Pucci one of *these* for his birthday instead of a dog! They don't shed, so your mother won't have to clean its hairs off the sofa—and you don't have to walk them, like with a dog. I think they're cheaper than a Chihuahua, too—and look how cute!"

"How do I get one, Dorinda? Do I have to go to Africa?"

"No, they have special pet stores here that buy them from breeders in New Zealand," Dorinda explains. "See, I've been kinda hoping Mrs. Bosco will let me get one for my brother Topwe, because he *really* wants a pet."

I think *Dorinda*'s the one pining for a pet, 'cuz that's how it is in *my* house. It's supposed to be for Pucci, but *I'm* the one who's all upset he isn't getting a pet for his birthday.

"Why do they call them hogs?" I ask, my curiosity all worked up. "They look more like porcupines."

"I guess 'cuz they're always looking for food or something," Dorinda guesses, shrugging her shoulders.

"Always looking for food, huh?" That sounds more like Dorinda's stepbrothers and stepsisters—especially Topwe. At Dorinda's adoption party Topwe ate the whole tray of candied yams topped with baked marshmallows before I even got a *whiff* of one!

Pobrecita, Dorinda. Poor thing . . . How is her family gonna find room for a pet, with thirteen people squeezed into a tiny apartment? She's even less likely to get a pet than *I* am!

"Lemme see that book," Bubbles asks curiously. She looks over our shoulders as we flip through the pages, oohing and aahing at the cute, furry, funny creatures. Most of the pictures show the hedgehogs crouched under woodpiles—obviously looking for their next meal.

I'm thinking Dorinda might be right . . . Maybe I *can* talk Mom into letting me get one of these for Pucci's birthday. I'll bet Mom wouldn't be allergic to those spines—they'd just stick her when she gets nasty, that's all!

"Maybe you can ask your mom to buy one for Pucci," Dorinda asks.

"*Yo no sé,*" I mumble, lapsing into Spanish unconsciously. I put my hand around my choker, and feel the metal letters which spell GROWL POWER. I need all the growl power I can muster up to ask Mami for anything. These days, it seems like all we do is fight—*la guerra Dominicana, está bien?* Heaving a sigh, I finger the letters on my choker again, and say proudly to Bubbles, "See, I told you this Wacky Glue was the move, *está bien?* It holds the letters on real well."

"You were right—it's the move," Bubbles says, nodding absentmindedly. She is still glued to the book, and *muy fascinada* with the pygmy pets.

At last, I see Derek and Mackerel bopping down the hallway in our direction. "Red Snapper Alert," I whisper softly, nudging Bubbles's arm.

She waves at Derek from down the hall, motioning for him to come over to us. Usually, we just ignore Derek (whom we call Red Snapper behind his back), but today we're happy to see him . . . and even Mackerel.

"Mr. Hambone, here you go. You are the proud owner of a Cheetah Girls choker," Bubbles says, handing him the choker, which we made extra wide just for him.

Derek examines the merchandise with a smile on his face, and fingers the shiny silver metal letters that spell SCEMO. "Oh, *that's* how you spell that word you're always calling me. Shame on *you*, Cheetah Girl. I dig it," Derek says, flashing his gold-toothed smile. (A lot of *la gente* where Abuela lives have gold teeth. *Cuatro yuks!*)

"Do you really like it?" I ask Derek proudly.

"Oh, yeah," he says, nodding his head. "You Cheetah Girls got skills, no doubt."

"No doubt on that tip," Mackerel says, nodding along, trying to get me to look at him—but it's too early in the morning for me to look at *his* snaggle-tooth smile.

We stand there waiting for Derek to whip out the duckets. Finally he gets the hint.

"Word, I guess it's time to dole out the duckets," he says, laughing and reaching into his deep-sea pockets.

We wait patiently as the Red Snapper retrieves a ten-dollar bill and hands it to Bubbles.

Wait a minute—I thought Bubbles told him the chokers cost *twenty* dollars!

"Did you get amnesia or something?"

Bubbles asks Derek on the *sarcástico* tip. "We said twenty dollars, my brutha."

"Yeah, well, we heard you was charging LaRonda ten dollars, *my sista*," Derek retorts, slapping Mackerel a high five.

Derek *always* has good comeback lines. I think that's why Bubbles doesn't like him— because he can snap better than she can, and Bubbles thinks she's the best—*la mejor*.

"Can't blame a Cheetah Girl for trying to get more 'pounce for the ounce,' now can you, Derek?" Bubbles snaps back, with a smirk on her face that says she's satisfied with *her* come-back line.

"No, but I hope you don't mind that the 'Red Snapper' is always gonna be 'off the hook!'" Derek says, heckling and slapping Mackerel a high five, like he is *supa*-satisfied with *his* snap.

How'd he know we call him the Red Snapper? Uh-oh. Somebody probably told him. Fashion Industries East peeps are like *telenovelas*, it seems—there is always some "drama" to watch.

"No, we don't mind, Derek—especially if you come back and buy another choker," I throw in, giggling. Bubbles doesn't always have to get the last word. Then—even though it kills me—I blurt out, "You know, Máckerel, *you* would look *tan coolio* with a choker, too!"

"Is that right?" he says, perking up and grinning ear to ear.

Oh, no! I don't want to see his *vampira* teeth—they're so crooked and pointy, they make me cringe!

Luckily, Dorinda steps up to the snap plate and says, "You two try to roll like you're the dynamic duo, right? Well, do it, duo! Buy another choker, joker!"

"*Ayiight.* I'll take one of them, too," Mackerel says—quietly, because he's kinda shy. That's when I notice that Mackerel's eyebrows are kinda arched high—just like High Priestess Abala Shaballa Cuckoo or whatever her name is. (She is the girlfriend of Aqua and Angie's father. We went over to the twins' apartment before we flew out to Los Angeles, and we had to drink this nasty "good luck" witches' brew she cooked up.)

Maybe Mackerel is a *vampira*, too, like her. You never how *la gente* are getting around these days—on broomsticks or the bus, *está bien?*

Mackerel gives Bubbles a five-dollar bill, then fishes around for more money out of his pocket.

"I got your back, Mack," Derek says, diving into his deep-sea pockets for more duckets. "Here you go, Cheetah Girl," he says, handing it to Galleria. Then he moves a little closer to her. "Maybe y'all wanna come to the fashion show at Times Square Tabernacle Church on Tuesday night. Tickets are ten dollars. It's for a good cause, and you'll get to see how a brutha works the runway, you know?"

"Maybe," Bubbles says, giving Dorinda and me a look, like, "We've got bigger fish to fry first." "We'll let you know, though, if we're gonna go with your flow, you know? But in the meantime, you know where to find *us*, if you need more product." She runs a finger slowly up between his choker and his neck, and Mr. DUH breaks into a goofy grin.

"Yeah, I'll look you up in the jiggy jungle!" he says, winking at Bubbles. "I gotta bounce— I've gotta go right now for a fitting. I'll check you by lunchtime, though."

"We'll save you some noodles. Toodles!" Bubbles says, waving behind her as the two of them go off, heckling like hyenas.

"He can heckle all he wants," Bubbles huffs, "'cuz we are about to get *paid*. We got *chokers*. What's *he* got to sell—*jokes*?"

"Word!" Do' Re Mi chuckles.

"What *boca grande* told Derek that we call him Red Snapper behind his back?" I ask, frowning.

"Probably that Kadeesha. They play basketball together sometimes. Can't blame her. She's probably trying to get Derek to ask her out. He's tall enough for her, right?" smirks Bubbles.

"What happened?" I chuckle, then I get my mind back on our business at hand. Turning to Dorinda, I say, "So listen. LaRonda's in my geography class. I can give her the choker and collect the duckets for us."

"Bet, *mamacita*. Better you, Do', than Miss Cuchifrito—she'd probably run off to some pygmy pet shops before we go to lunch," Bubbles says. "And you'd better check out Oakland on the map today!"

Bubbles *would* bring up the little "boo-boo" I

made in California. While we were backstage, getting ready for our showcase, I started talking to one of the other groups who were performing—CMG, the Cash Money Girls—and they said they were from Oakland. Me with my *boca grande*, I asked, "Where it that?"

How was I supposed to know Oakland is in California? I mean, I'm representing the East Coast, *está bien*?

"I bet *you* didn't know where it was either," I shoot back in protest.

"Yeah, well, I sure wouldn't have let Miss Abrahamma Lincoln in on that tip, that's all I'm saying," Bubbles says with a grin, then waves her hand in my face.

"I wonder which one of *them* writes the raps for their songs," I say, changing the subject. Bubbles has got me annoyed now, and I figure it's as good a time as any to bring up my new pet peeve. "Maybe they write them *together*?"

"Why?" Bubbles asks, smirking.

"*Porqué*—because—I don't know. Maybe *we* could write songs together," I blurt out.

There. I said it. Why *can't* I write songs for the Cheetah Girls, too? How come Bubbles is the only one who gets to write songs?

"We *who*?" Bubbles asks, like she doesn't get what I'm talking about.

"*Me* and *you, está bien?*"

"Chuchie . . . maybe you should stick with what you do best—"

"What happened? How do you know what I do best?" I ask, getting flustered.

"Chuchie, the bell's gonna ring for homeroom. And then we have to walk to first period before I can take off these wet shoes." Bubbles is showing me how exasperated she is. But I know it's just a way for her to blow me off. She doesn't want to talk about letting me write songs with her.

"One thing you did really well—taking doggy poo off my shoe," Bubbles snaps, putting me in my place. "Now I'm walking around like Flipper!" Bubbles starts walking to her desk, waddling like she's got fins on her feet. Some peeps look up like she's a little cuckoo, but I'm used to that. It's not like we're walking around unnoticed with all the cheetah-licious outfits we wear.

"So what? It's not my fault the faucets in the bathroom are older than the Dominican Day Parade!" I call after her.

"Can we stop talking about it now, please?" she says, sitting down and opening up her cheetah backpack. "By the time we sell these chokers, it'll be time for a markdown sale or something!" she mumbles, not looking at me.

"*Está bien*," I say, giving in. I never win fights with Bubbles. She *always* has the last word. Why am I even worrying about writing songs, anyway? We don't even have a record deal! We'll be lucky if we don't end up headlining karaoke clubs and singing "Wanna-be Stars in the Jiggy Jungle" for the rest of our lives!

Chapter 4

Bubbles and I are sitting in homeroom class, turning our heads really slow, so everyone can check out our chokers—especially Keisha Jackson.

I'll never forget what Keisha did on the first day of the semester: our homeroom teacher, Mr. Drezform, asked the class if any of us spoke another language besides English. A few students raised their hands—including me and Bubbles, of course.

Keisha cut her eyes at us, like we were telling fib-eronis or something. Then, after class, she had the nerve to come up to Bubbles and ask her if she *really* spoke Italian. So now I'm not feeling Miss Keisha, *está bien?*

Luckily, a few students smile at me as I crane my neck at them. I smile back, showing off the choker. Then I turn to my right and say hi to Daisy Duarte, who is supa-chili—and also Dominican, like me.

"*Ay, qué bonita!* Your choker is so cute!" she exclaims, checking out the "product."

"My crew and I make them," I say proudly. "Support a Cheetah Girl—come on, buy one, Daisy!" I egg her on, because we're really cool like that with each other.

"How much?" Daisy asks, amused to the max.

For a second I hesitate. Then I realize, Bubbles has already gotten busted once for pricehiking—by Derek Hambone, no less. So I figure we'd better chill, and I blurt out, "Ten dollars. *Está poco*, okay?"

"*Está bien*," Daisy says, her eyes lighting up.

I motion to Bubbles, who whips out a Cheetah Girls choker from her backpack and hands it to me. Since it's my sale, I pass the choker to Daisy.

Daisy looks as happy as my mom does at a garage sale. Her eyes are glistening, like she knows she's gotten a really good bargain, *está bien?* Daisy forks over ten dollars with pleasure, then snaps the choker onto her neck like it's a trophy.

"How does it look?" she asks me, pushing her long, wavy hair behind her shoulders to show off the choker.

"*La dopa*—and fresh as a Daisy!" I respond proudly, then hurriedly fold the crisp ten-dollar bill into my cheetah wallet. I stuff the wallet into my backpack before Mr. Drezform takes attendance.

"Talk to you later!" I whisper, pinching Bubbles under the chair. I feel so much better already!

I guess it was kinda hard, adjusting to being back in school after our dream trip to La La Land. We got to lie in a pool, perform for the bigwigs—and I even met this publicity executive from Def Duck Records at the showcase. He said that I reminded him of Kahlua Alexander, their biggest artist!

I am lost in my own *Telemundo* channel, when I hear Mr. Drezform call my name *loudly*. Bubbles pokes me really hard.

"Here!" I yell, then sit back in my chair and take out the pygmy hedgehog book. I wonder if the little hoglets only make tiny poopoos in the kitty litter box. Otherwise, you can forget it—*olvídate, está bien?* Mom is even worse about odors than I am—unless they're coming out of very expensive perfume bottles!

When attendance is over, I jump up because I have to go to the bathroom before first period. I smile at Daisy and say good-bye, then tell Bubbles I'll meet her in math class.

As soon as the bell rings, I get up to make a mad dash out the classroom door. But all of a sudden, I hear Keisha Jackson yelling at Bubbles.

"Yo, Galleria, I think you dropped something," Keisha says with a smirk, handing her—gasp—the silver letter "L" from Bubbles's Cheetah Girl choker!

Ay, Dios mío! I think I'm going to faint! Quickly, I put my hand around my neck. *Gracias gooseness*—thank goodness—I still have all my letters.

Bubbles snatches the silver letter from Keisha's hand and puts it in her pocket, like it's no biggie—but I know she is *goospitating*.

"Galleria, you know what? It doesn't look too bad without the 'L'—'Grow Power!' I like it!" Keisha says, heckling. Then she says, in a real loud voice, "I heard you and Chanel tell Daisy that *you* made the chokers?"

I am so humiliated, I wish I could do an abra-cadabra on the spot and disappear! "Yes, *we* made them," Bubbles whimpers. Her face has turned five shades of my favorite color—red.

"Maybe you'd better tell Daisy, before hers falls apart next period," Keisha says. Sucking her teeth, she walks off, like she's a designer herself or something. Come on—she majors in fashion merchandising, just like we do. *Qué bobada*. Phony baloney!

I stand next to Bubbles, shifting back and forth on my feet because I have to go to the bathroom really bad. But I'm not moving until Bubbles does. "I guess that Wacky Glue went wacky, Chuchie," Bubbles says, sucking her teeth.

"What happened?" I stammer. "Don't blame it on me!" We stand there frozen, contemplating whether we should say anything to Daisy. I can tell we are both thinking the same thing— *Run for the hills with the bills!*

A few of the students look at us while they're pushing their way out of class, but we don't move.

"Should I tell Daisy?" I finally ask.

"Nah. Hers is probably fine," Bubbles says. "But we'd better check with Do' Re Mi before she gives LaRonda her choker!" Dorinda's homeroom is just down the hall.

When we get outside into the hallway, I suddenly feel dizzy. I lean against the corridor wall because I feel like I'm going to faint. "Bubbles," I mumble, "what are we gonna do?"

When I hear Daisy's shrill voice calling my name, I realize the curtain is about to come down on our little *charada*. One look at Daisy's face, and I definitely know our off-Broadway production is closed for renovations until further notice!

"Um, Chanel, I think there is a problem with my choker," Daisy says apologetically, handing it to me. "The snaps popped off—I'm sorry, but I couldn't find them—I don't know where they fell. This thing just came off my neck. I didn't pull on it or anything!"

"*Está bien*, Daisy, no *te preocupas*," I say in Spanish, because I don't want everybody to hear about our catastrophe! "Don't worry about it."

"Can you give me my ten dollars back, please?" Daisy asks me nicely.

"Oh, sure," I say, wincing. I scrounge around in my cheetah backpack for my cheetah wallet. I'm so nervous that my keys, my books, and all my other junk fall out of my backpack! The crowds going both ways through the hall start kicking my stuff all over the place!

"It's right there," Daisy says, trying to be helpful and pointing to my wallet, which is under the only notebook that hasn't fallen out of my backpack.

"Ooh, you're right," I say, giggling nervously. "Here. I'm sorry. I'll make you another one."

"Oh, that's okay," she says. She gives me a smile and shrugs. "Sorry. They're cute, though. See you later." And she turns and leaves, in a big hurry to get out of that embarrassing situation.

Daisy will probably *never* buy anything from me as long as I live. I swear, *Te juro*. It's only right, after all. And she'll probably tell everybody from here to the *barrio* that the Cheetah Girls are not ready for prime time—just broken-down cubs trying to get some grub!

I look pleadingly at Bubbles, but she gives me a look like she's gonna wring my neck.

After Daisy leaves, she hisses, "You were the one who said the Wacky Glue would be strong enough to hold the letters. Obviously it isn't."

Stammering, I point out, "Yeah, but that's not why the snap closures came undone in the back, *está bien?* It's not *all* my fault."

"Yeah, well, obviously, we didn't know how to work the snap machine either," Galleria admits, softening.

Fighting the tears welling up inside, I take a deep breath, then hightail it with Bubbles to find Do' Re Mi before she goes to her next class and gives LaRonda the soon-to-be-broken-down choker.

When I see Do' Re Mi walking toward *us,* with a look on her face like she got hit with something, I know it's too late.

"I don't know what happened," she says, shaking her head, embarrassed. "The letters came off LaRonda's choker! I had to give her back the ten dollars." Do' Re Mi hands Bubbles the choker, like it's a squashed mouse. "We couldn't find all the letters that came off, either."

"I know," I say, feeling my breath leave my body like I'm in a seance.

"How did you know?" Do' Re Mi asks, puzzled.

"Look at this one," I huff. I pull the choker I sold to Daisy out of my jacket pocket. "The snaps came off this one, *and* the letters came off Bubbles's choker!"

"Word? What are we gonna do, Galleria?" Do' Re Mi whines, rolling her eyes to the ceiling. I know exactly what she's thinking before she even says it. "If Derek's choker starts to fall apart, we are burnt toast!"

"I know—but let's just go with the flow," Bubbles says, trying to act *coolio*. "Obviously, the Wacky Glue had a wack attack."

"Don't blame it on Chanel, Galleria. It's *our* fault, too," Do' Re Mi says, hanging on to the straps of her backpack.

I stand there, stunned. This is the first time Dorinda has ever stuck up for me. One day, me and Bubbles had a big fight, right on the sidewalk outside of my house. Bubbles stormed off, and Dorinda went running after her and left me standing there on the sidewalk.

"Oh, squash it, Do', I know!" Bubbles snaps, then rolls her eyes at me.

"I'm sorry, okay?" I hiss.

"That's cool, we'll just go with the flow—like I said," Bubbles retorts.

We stand there, silent, trying to plan our next move, but I should've known we weren't getting off the hambone hook that easy. All of a sudden, we hear Derek rolling down the hallway, calling us out.

As soon as he has us in his sights, he moans, "Yo, Cheetah Girls, your product is *fowl* like a nearsighted *owl*!"

"Tell me this isn't happening!" Bubbles moans. "I wish I could use Wacky Glue on Derek's trap!"

Bubbles tries to squash the situation. "Derek, hold up—"

But Derek isn't having it. "Cheetah Girl, what you trying to do to me? You got jokes or something?" Derek asks, handing Bubbles the choker we sold him earlier.

"W-what do you mean?" Bubbles asks him, stuttering. We all stand there, pretending we don't know a tropical storm like Furious Flo is blowing our way—again.

"You *know* what I mean," Derek says, sucking on his lollipop, and posturing like he's ready to pounce—on us. "I'm on my way to

English class, where I'm supposed to be dropping knowledge, and instead I'm dropping letters from the alphabet—like I'm Daffy Duck, or Elmo on *Sesame Street*!" Derek resumes sucking on his lollipop. He's waiting for Bubbles to explain.

Cheez whiz, I'm thinking, *someone musta told Derek that we call him Daffy Duck, too!* Dorinda is the one who thought of that one.

Galleria hasn't opened her mouth, so Derek starts in again. "All I wanna say is, if this is the best joke you got, I got jokes for you, too—but you're gonna have to pay me just to hear them. In the meantime, you can gimme back my ten dollars!"

"Derek, I'm sorry. I didn't mean to sell you a wack choker. It just happened," Bubbles whimpers. She reaches into her cheetah wallet to give him back his ten dollars.

"Word, Derek, we didn't know what we were doing," Do' Re Mi offers, trying to be super-*simpático*.

"Mack, did you hear an echo or something?" Derek says, looking at Mackerel, then looking around like he can't figure out who's talking. Finally, he looks down at Do' Re Mi. "Oh, shortie! Was that you? You got something to say to me?"

"Derek, don't go there—" Bubbles tries to counter, but he cuts her off.

"No. Shame on *you*, Cheetah Girl, 'cuz I'm not the 'shay-mo' you think I am. As a matter of fact, *you* are. And you'd better go back to Finger Painting 101 before you start acting like you 'all that'—ayiight?" He throws the metal letters that fell off his choker on the ground in front of us. "'Cuz you definitely got an 'F' on your report card for social studies."

"*Awwriight*," seconds Mackerel, handing the choker he bought back to Bubbles, too—and taking *another* ten dollars from her.

"You gotta have skills to pay the bills, Cheetah Girls—not jokes!" Derek yells all the way down the hallway, heckling with Mackerel. The two of them sound like hyenas, heading back to the hills to pounce on more innocent prey.

"Let's bounce," Bubbles mumbles, leading us toward the exit. "We're gonna have to be late for next period. We need to get outside and bounce from this situation."

* * *

"We're definitely gonna have to regroup," Do' Re Mi says, sighing, as we sit on the steps in front of the school.

"Regroup?" Bubbles retorts. "I'm *never* going back to school, *ever* again!"

The three of us sit in complete silence for what seems like hours. Then I turn to Bubbles and say, "Remember that time *Madrina* told us about the first cat suits she made?"

"No," Bubbles says quietly. "What'd she say?"

"She said she made them so small they didn't even fit an alley cat," I say, repeating what *Madrina* had told me. "She said she had a lot of problems when she started her business. She even had trouble fitting the customers, because she didn't really know what she was doing.

"I remember my mom thought it was all a big joke," I continue, "'cuz she didn't believe that *Madrina* was ever gonna be a real designer. I still remember the big fight they had about it when Bubbles and I were little," I tell Dorinda.

"I guess we're gonna have to figure out how to make the chokers so they don't fall apart," she says, trying to be helpful.

"I really do feel bad, like it's my fault," I tell my crew.

"Chuchie, just chill," Bubbles says. "We were moving too fast on the eager-beaver tip—trying to floss *and* make everybody proud of us—especially our moms. Right?"

"Right!" Dorinda and I agree.

"Well, I guess we don't have anything better to do than keep trying—at least until we hear if we got a record deal, huh?" Bubbles says. She puts her hands to her temples, like the weight of the world is on her head. "Okay, let's regroup. But I'll tell you one thing—I wish I never had to look at Derek Hambone and his gold tooth again as long as I live."

"Or Mackerel," I say with a smirk, then take a deep breath. "But I guess we have a *lot* to learn."

"And we might as well face the factos—we are definitely in the *dog pound* for now," Bubbles says.

Suddenly, I blurt out, "Woof, there it is!" Next thing you know, I'm laughing so hard, I am doubled over in pain, holding my stomach.

Dorinda and Bubbles join me in a giggle-filled chorus of "Woof, there it is! Woof, there it is!" We just keep saying it, over and over again, because we don't know any of the other words to the song.

But Bubbles soon takes care of that. Right there on the front steps of Fashion Industries East High, for all the sidewalk passersby to hear, she leads us by singing the rest of the song, and we repeat the words after her:

> *"It takes five*
> *To make the Cheetah Girls be*
> *Ah, yeah, can't you see*
> *That they're rocking on a thing*
> *Called the M.I.C.*
> *The M.I.C., well that's a microphone*
> *And when they rock it to the beat*
> *It's rocked to the doggy bone.*
>
> *Woof, there it is!*
> *Woof, there it is!*
> *Woof, there it is!"*

By now, a small crowd of people on the street has joined us, and they're singing along! This is what I love. This is what we all love. *The beat.*

The beat is what brings us to our feet. *The beat is why we're together—forever!*

After we finish and settle down, I say, "We've *gotta* get that record deal."

Bubbles just sighs. "Yeah—a record deal, or at least a square meal. Come on, y'all—we're missing class. I guess singing is our thing, but when it comes to making chokers, we're just a bunch of jokers."

Chapter 5

By the end of the school day, Bubbles has finally calmed down. Dorinda and I spent the whole lunch period talking some sense into her. When school lets out, we hit the subway, heading for the Toto in New York factory in Brooklyn—again.

"Don't be a joker, G, let's go make some chokers," Dorinda chuckles. That's right—we've talked Galleria into trying again!

Aqua and Angie have agreed to meet us there. We paged them during lunch period, and set it all up.

The twins are getting very brave these days. Usually, we have to meet them at a subway station, and go together as a group to places—

because they don't know New York very well, and are afraid of traveling by themselves.

But since this is the second time they are going to the Toto in New York factory, they are willing to take a chance. We're hoping they won't get on the wrong train and end up back in Houston (their hometown, which has the best Cajun crawfish that side of Texas, if you let them tell it)!

The first thing *we* do when we get to the factory is "eat humble pie." After all, our mission, if we choose to accept it, is to find out what went ka-flooey with our chokers!

As usual, my *madrino* is so understanding about the whole *catástrofe* that he makes us laugh.

"Rome wasn't built in a day, my sweet *cara*." He chuckles as he greets us.

"Hi, Mr. Garibaldi," Dorinda says, smiling. You can tell she likes *Madrino* a lot, too—but then, who doesn't?

Shortly after we get situated, the fabulous Walker twins arrive—in one piece—and ready for a helping of Rosita's famous baked ziti. Rosita is the head pattern maker at the factory, and every Monday she brings a tray of baked ziti to work.

"This is goo-ood," Angie tells Rosita between mouthfuls.

"We *iz* so glad nothing happened to *our* chokers," Aqua pipes up.

"Well, that's because the two of you are just *so special*," Bubbles hisses at them jokingly. I give the twins a wink, just to make sure they know Galleria's joking.

Rosita is especially happy to see Bubbles. She runs over to her and pinches her cheeks, then runs to the microwave to heat up some more ziti.

Madrino and his employees always cook big, fat feasts for lunch or dinner if they have to work late, and today is no exception. I feel so at home here, and I'm so used to all the different smells in the factory. First, there's always a pot of baked ziti or something bubbling in the microwave oven. Then, there's the sharp smell of cleaning fluid floating around, or the fresh heat from the clothing steamer machines. On top of that is the faint smell of sewing machine oil—because the machines are always purring softly in the background.

After we eat, Bubbles tries to be patient while her dad shows us how to use the snap contraption the *right* way.

"Oh, word," Dorinda exclaims, opening and closing the snaps on a strip of suede. She is completely fascinated with this contraption. Lucky for the rest of us, too—even after *Madrino*'s little lesson, Dorinda is the only one of us who can manage to put the snaps on the suede fabric so they don't look lumpy.

What's really bothering me is, why did the letters fall off so easily? "*Madrino*," I ask him, "how come the letters don't stay on? I thought the Wacky Glue was strong enough to hold anything!"

"Chanel, *cara*, you cannot always believe the advertisements!" Mr. Garibaldi tries to explain.

"I think Mr. Garibaldi means 'don't believe the hype,'" Dorinda says knowingly.

"*Si, cara*, that's right," *Madrino* says. Clasping his fingers together in order to demonstrate, he says, "In order for the fabric to hold the letters, you should sew two strips of the choker together—stitching it around here." He shows us with a strip of fabric. "Then use a glue like Duco to put the letters on. That Wacky Glue stuff is for amateurs."

Wow. This whole choker thing is gonna take a lot more work than we thought!

"Don't worry, Bubbles. Maybe by next year, we'll be able to make the chokers by ourselves!" Angie jokingly tells Bubbles. But I don't think Bubbles finds it funny, because she has her mouth stuck out. The rest of us just keep quiet while *Madrino* continues with his demonstration.

Maybe next semester I should sign up for Accessories Workshop. . . . I think that's what Derek was really trying to say—that we should really learn how to do something before we jump into the "players' pond," as Bubbles calls it. Derek sure made his point when he threw the metal letters on the floor! I'll never forget Bubbles's face when he did that!

"Okay, now we've got six chokers to sell," Bubbles says as we head back to Manhattan on the subway together. "But we'd better come back another time and make some more chokers—just to be on the safe side."

"*Tutti frutti* wit' me," jokes Aqua, as she gives us all a big hug. The twins are off to have dinner with their father and his girlfriend, High Priestess Abala Shaballa Cuckoo for Cocoa Puffs, or whatever her name is.

It's Raining Benjamins

Abala claims she is a high priestess from some faraway place in Hexagonia, where cuckoos come from. I guess she must be telling the truth, because she is as cuckoo as they come—and I am used to *brujería, santería, oju,* and any other kind of witchcraft you can think of, because I'm Dominican, *está bien?* And we've got it all down there!

Anyway, the twins, their dad, and the High Priestess are all going to Mr. Walker's new boss's house, so they have to get home on time. Mr. Walker just started this big new job in marketing. He is working on some new roach spray campaign—or maybe it's fleas . . . I can't remember.

"What you up to this afternoon, Miss Chanel?" Angie asks me. "You working at Toto?"

I work at *Madrina*'s store three afternoons a week, until I can pay Mom back for the money I "borrowed" on her card. But Monday afternoons I'm free. Still, that doesn't mean I'm hanging around the house all day and night. I've got other things going—with me, it's always something.

"I'm running in the Junior Gobbler Race next

week, and I've gotta train for it," I explain. Of course, I know everybody is gonna start laughing at me as soon as they get wind of this, but that's okay—*está bien*. Let them laugh.

"What on earth is the Junior Gobbler Race?" Angie wants to know. She's holding on to a pole with one hand as the subway car rocks back and forth. With her free hand, she's cleaning her teeth with a toothpick.

"It's a race for kids in Central Park," I explain. "You're gonna stab yourself with that toothpick. Cut it out—you're making me crazy!"

"How old you gotta be to run in the race?" Angie asks, putting away the toothpick, *gracias gooseness*.

"They have two divisions for kids," I explain. "The race for the little kids is five blocks. For kids ten to fourteen years old, it's about one mile." I'm hoping the twins will run the race with me. But no—the only thing they like about turkey is eating it.

"We would love to come running with you— but tonight is very important for our daddy," Aqua explains. "You know he got that new marketing job, and he is working real hard coming up with a new bug spray campaign."

"I hope his boss ain't got no roaches in his house!" Angie adds.

"Not everybody has got roaches here, Aqua and Angie!" Dorinda exclaims, offended. I guess Dorinda is embarrassed because the Boscos' apartment *does* have roaches. We never told Dorinda, but when we were at her house, Aqua got real upset when she saw all the roaches in her kitchen. "Who invited *them* to the party," I remember her saying.

"Dorinda, do *you* want to come running with me today?" I ask, putting my arm around her shoulders. She is kinda athletic, like me, and she is the best dancer in the group—even though she never studied ballet, like I did.

"What do you get if you win?" Dorinda asks.

"A ten-pound turkey!" I say, giggling. Dorinda *loves* to eat, and *Dios* knows her family could use a big, fat turkey, to feed all those hungry foster kids.

I wonder if Mrs. Bosco cooks a big meal for Thanksgiving, like we do? Maybe we should invite Dorinda to spend Thanksgiving with us . . . Me and Mom usually go over to Bubbles's house to eat. *Madrina* cooks enough food to feed Cuba. I guess there'd be enough for Mrs. Bosco and her whole houseful!

"Okay," Dorinda says shrugging her shoulders. "We have to run anyway, for our exercise program, right? I might as well try to win the turkey."

"Yep," I say, looking at Bubbles to see how she reacts. See, *Madrina* has us all on a program. For one thing, we have to run—three times a week, to build endurance. This will also help keep our vocal cords in shape, she tells us. It's like a stamina thing, so when we perform we don't get tired, *entiendes?* And so we have enough breath power to hit all the high notes. Mom usually runs with us since she loves to exercise.

Bubbles doesn't care, though. She hates running. I remember when Mom went away to Paris with Mr. Tycoon, Bubbles convinced all of us Cheetah Girls to slack off from our running training. When Mom got back, she was pretty annoyed at all of us!

When Dorinda and I get off the subway at my stop, Bubbles throws me a kiss good-bye, winks, and says, "Gobble, gobble, Miss Cuchifrito!"

* * *

As usual, Pucci is home watching television. Since his birthday is on Saturday, I'm trying to be nice to him, but that sure takes a lot of patience. When he comes out of his room, I ask him, "Pucci, you wanna train with me for the Junior Gobbler race?"

"No, stupid, I'm a Cuckoo Cougar!" He snipes at me, shooting an imaginary machine gun, then plops down at the kitchen table with a chocolate chip cookie and a glass of milk. In two seconds, there's a huge stain on his fighter-pilot T-shirt.

"Wipe your shirt, you *bugaboo*," I hiss at him. Pucci is right about one thing—he's cuckoo, all right.

"He's always watching that stupid cartoon on television," I explain to Dorinda as we change into our running shoes. "Now he's even talking about starting a Cougar Club in school!"

At least he looks cuter now that he's starting to let his hair grow back. "Bubbles used to call Pucci 'Eight ball,' "I tell Dorinda, "because he looked so funny with a bald head."

"Where's your mom?" Dorinda asks, kinda motioning me to get up the nerve and pop the Pucci question to her.

"Probably in the den," I say, making a comical grimace in response. "I'll go see. I'd better talk to her while I still have the nerve to ask her about Pucci's pet." I mouth the last two words silently, motioning to the other room where my poot-butt brother is. He has ears like an elephant, he's so nosy.

To help support my case with Mom, I unzip my cheetah backpack and take out the book on African pygmy hedgehogs.

"*Oink, oink,*" I say, giggling, to Dorinda. "Wait here."

Bending around the corner of our loft apartment, I pad quietly to the den, and see Mom seated in front of the computer. I haven't seen her working at the computer for quite some time. Not since her book about the history of black models—*They Shoot Models, Don't They?*—was published this fall . . . and flopped. Well, it didn't exactly "flop," but Mom wasn't happy with the reviews she got, if you catch my meaning. As she puts it, "What do critics know about models, anyway?"

"*Qué tú haces, Mamí?*" I ask her curiously. "What'cha doin'?"

"Oh, I'm trying to get my thoughts together

for this new book idea I have, about the rise and fall of oil tycoons and their girlfriends. It's called, *It's Raining Tycoons*," Mom says, running her fingers through her ponytail.

"'*It's Raining Tycoons*,'" I repeat, amused, wondering where she would get the inspiration for something like *that*! (That's a joke—*una broma, está bien?*) "I like that, *Mamí*. Are *you* gonna write it?"

Mom looks at me, really annoyed. I feel like a *babosa*. I'm supposed to be nice to her so she'll let me pick out a pet for Pucci—not get on her nerves! See, I'm not supposed to know *Mamí* used a ghost writer—not that kind of ghost but someone who helps with writing a book. I have such a *boca grande*! What a big mouth!

"I'm looking at several writers, actually," she says, sniffing. "But who knows? I may actually do more work on this one. You know what they say—if you want something done right, do it yourself."

"*Está bien!*" I say, smiling. "Um, *Mamí* . . . 'member what you said about getting Pucci a Chihuahua for his birthday?"

"Yes, I remember that—and *you* can *forget* it!" Mom says curtly.

Now I can feel my cheeks turning five shades of red. I start stammering, "*Pero—*"

"But, *nada*," Mom says, finishing my sentence for me. "End of discussion!"

As a last resort, I shove the book into Mom's hand. I know she can't resist something as cute as these little creatures, any more than anybody else can. I just know it. "Aren't they cute?" I say, kinda casual.

"*Qué es esto?*" Mom asks, but she doesn't seem amused. "What are these things?"

"They're hedgehogs?" I answer, like I'm asking a question.

"And what is *that?*" Mom asks in a softer tone. I take the bait, because I figure maybe she'll listen to me now.

"They're animals you can have, like, um, a little pet, I explain. "Much easier than a dog!"

"They look like porcupines," Mom retorts.

"No, *Mamí*, they're not porcupines. Their closest relatives are moonrats. Um, they're members of a group of animals known as *insectivora*," I respond, trying to sound smart, like Dorinda.

"Hmmm. They're very cute," Mom says, then hands me back the book.

"They *are*, right?" I ask, my eyes brightening, because now I know I've got a fighting chance! "Maybe we could get one for Pucci for his, um, birthday?"

"No!" she says, annoyed. "Didn't you hear me the first time? After you get tired of playing with this whatever-it-is, the only person who is gonna end up taking care of it is *me*."

I am so mad at her, I could shake her! NO!— that's all she ever says to anything I want!

"*Está bien*," I moan, feeling completely defeated. "I'm going running with Dorinda."

Storming out of the den, I realize that I didn't even ask her what she *is* getting Pucci for his birthday. I don't even care anymore! Whatever it is, she's not telling, and I'm not going to ask her. And I guess I'm supposed to be getting him *nada*—since all I have is *nada* money.

Dorinda takes one look at my face, and she knows what time it is. Time to run and run and *run*. . . .

"Don't be mad at your mom, Chanel," Dorinda says, trying to console me, as we cross the inter-section of Forty-second Street and First Avenue.

I look over at the United Nations building, with all the hundreds of countries' flags blowing in the wind. They look so pretty . . . . I look for the flags of the Dominican Republic and Cuba—Abuela's and Daddy's countries.

Then I turn away, and think about what I'm going to get Pucci for his birthday. "I can't think of anything else to get him," I moan to Dorinda. "No more of those stupid Whacky Babies, that's for sure. If he gets one more of those things, I'm throwing them all out of the window!"

"You're buggin'," Dorinda says, smiling because she understands. I don't know how she puts up with all those foster brothers and sisters of hers. I would go *cuckoo* for Cocoa Puffs. I guess having just one brother isn't so bad—even if that brother is as big a pain as Pucci!

Chapter 6

After Dorinda goes home, all the way "uptown, baby," I shower and change into some clean clothes, but I'm still fuming about Mom and her selfishness. She was just trying to show off in front of *Madrina* and my crew that day in the store. Why else would she have said she was gonna let us get a Chihuahua if she didn't really mean it?

I put on my favorite red wool skirt with the big gold safety pin, a red turtleneck, and tights. I pick up the receiver of the red princess phone in my bedroom and call my dad's girlfriend, Princess Pamela, to let her know I'm on my way to her Psychic Palace.

She's taking the braids out of my hair tonight, even though my mother doesn't know it. By the time I hang up the receiver, I'm giggling my head off, because Princess Pamela always makes me laugh. She's so sweet to me.

That's when I decide to wear the Tiffany diamond earring studs Princess Pamela gave me as a present. Mom almost cracked her facial mask the first time she saw them sparkling in my earlobes. She made me swear that I would *never* take any more presents from Princess Pamela.

Well, maybe I will, and maybe I won't. I mean, Mom doesn't keep her word, so why should I, *está bien?* She promised to get me—I mean Pucci—a Chihuahua, and now she won't even get him a pygmy hedgehog!

I go to my musical jewelry box, and take out the little blue box I keep hidden in the bottom. Inside the little box are the tiny diamond studs. I hold them up to the light, admiring them— the most beautiful things I own—then I stick them in my ears.

Just because *Mom* doesn't want a pet, why shouldn't *Pucci* have one? Mom uses the excuse that she's "allergic to animals," and that she'll have to take care of it all by herself—but I don't believe her about either one. She's just being selfish. I'll bet if Mr. Tycoon bought her a poodle or something as a present, she would be cooing like a coconut, all the way from here to Paree—a.k.a. Paris, France!

I go into the kitchen to get some orange juice. I don't even care if Mom sees that I'm wearing the diamond studs.

Pucci bounces into the kitchen. "You'd better not drink my Burpy Soda," he says, flinging open the refrigerator and grabbing a can.

"I don't even want your stupid soda, *burphead*," I grumble. Mom lets Pucci order Burpy Soda off the Internet, but what he really needs is a muzzle. I hope she gets him one for his birthday!

"Daddy's coming on Saturday for my birthday," Pucci brags, then starts dancing around.

"Aren't *you* lucky?" I say, grimacing. What I wish is that Princess Pamela could come over here with Daddy and Abuela—but that's never gonna happen, because Mom would get so upset her face would crack, and she'd have to get a face-lift!

"I wonder what *Papí* got me for my birthday,"

Pucci says, raising his eyebrows like *el diablo* and making faces.

"I'm sure it's something *muy preciosa*, Pucci," I say, putting away the orange juice before I pour it over his head. "Bye, *Mamí*, wherever you are," I yell, as I head out the door, and over to Princess Pamela's Psychic Palace, which happens to be just around the corner. (That's how Dad met her—he went over there for a haircut and a palm reading one day when he was sick and tired of fighting with Mom.)

Now I feel like a *babosa*. Why was I feeling guilty about going to Princess Pamela's to get my braids taken out?

Well . . . that's not exactly why I'm going, actually. I'm going to Princess Pamela's because I love her, and because she makes me feel happy about everything that I'm trying to do with the Cheetah Girls.

"Chanel!" Princess Pamela coos when I come in the door. That is what I love about my dad's girlfriend—she always makes me feel like she has won the lottery when she sees my face.

"Come, sit. I *brought* just for you the best caviar I can find," Princess Pamela coos in her syrupy, heavy Romanian accent, which I love.

She shoves a little silver spoon filled with little black alien eggs at my face. "Come, try, *pleez*."

I put the teeny-weeny alien goofballs on my tongue. Caviar tastes really different, kinda like cold *bacalao*—salted Spanish codfish—but not *exactly*.

"*Dahling*, you like?" Princess Pamela asks, her big brown eyes opening wide.

"Yeah," I say, giggling. "Salty."

"Pleez, eat some *polenta*, too," she commands me. "What I could get for this food on the Romanian black market, I cannot tell you! But, ah, those were the days."

"What do you mean?" I ask curiously, sopping up some of the Romanian potato bread, which Princess Pamela says she makes just like her mother. I love when Princess Pamela tells me stories about "the old country," which in her case is Transylvania, Romania—home of Count Dracula.

"When my country was Communist, we had such a black market—you could make a *k-e-e-l-i-n-g* if you had the right items to sell. Now, we have no Communism, no democracy, and everyone is *very* confused. Ah, *beeneh*, very well," Princess Pamela says wistfully.

I sit in the beauty parlor chair, and listen to the Romanian gypsy music wafting in the background. I try to relax, even though I feel really tense.

"What is troubling you, my booti-ful Chanel?" Princess Pamela asks me, as she takes out my braids with her nimble fingers.

I tell her the whole pygmy hedgehog story, hoping that she will have a solution for me. After all, Princess Pamela *is* a psychic, and she knows how to tell if your dreams will come true.

"I don't see the furry creature with the—how do you say—" she says, scrunching up her face so I can understand what she's trying to say.

"Whiskers?" I ask, giggling.

"Riight, *beeneh*, good. I don't see the furry creature with the whiskers coming under your pillow while you sleep—but, ah, thiz is good, becuz, some of the furrrry creee-tures make you frightened, no?"

She smiles at me, and I try to smile back—even though I'm crushed that she doesn't see any cute little pygmy hedgehogs in my future.

"*Beeneh*, good, but, something better is coming for you. You don't have to worry, Chanel,"

Princess Pamela says, her eyes twinkling the way they always do when she knows a secret.

I remember she told me once to watch out for the animals—and sure enough, Mr. "Jackal" Johnson, our so-called manager at the time, turned out to be a predator in a pinstriped suit, *está bien?*

"How is your mother, anyway?" Princess Pamela asks, while she twists my hair in sections.

"Well, I guess it's raining tycoons," I giggle.

"It's raining tycoons—what does that mean, Chanel?" Princess Pamela asks, amused.

"I don't know—I guess everything is okay with Mr. Tycoon, alrighty, alrooty."

"Ah, *beeneh,* I see," Princess Pamela says. Then she starts humming to the music.

"I hope you're right, though, Princess Pamela. I hope something good is coming, because we haven't heard anything yet from the record company," I say with a sigh.

Then I look in the mirror at my new hairdo. My hair is all wavy and loose now—it kinda looks like Bubbles's, but not as wild. "I like it," I coo to Princess Pamela, then hug her good-bye.

"*La revedere, cara,*" she says. "You will hear something verrry soon, I promise."

If Princess Pamela's predictions are any-where near as good as her hairdos, then I won't be searching "somewhere over the rainbow" much longer. I practically float all the way home, daydreaming about us, the Cheetah girls, singing—and furry creatures with little whiskers.

When I lie down on my pillow that night, I drift into a dream. I see lots of money falling, falling from the sky. Bubbles is in the dream, too. She has an umbrella, and we are trying to grab all the money that is falling from the sky.

Then we start fighting over the money. Bubbles is trying to grab it from me, because, she screams, "You don't deserve it!"

Suddenly it starts raining, and we're both crying because we're getting all wet. The money is getting wet, too—and Bubbles starts screaming that our dreams are ruined, and how it's all my fault!

It starts raining so hard that we both give up grabbing for the falling money. We struggle to get under the same umbrella, to keep from get-ting wet. All of a sudden, the umbrella starts lifting us up off the ground, and we're flying through the air! I start getting scared, but Bubbles says, "Just hang on real tight, and we won't have anything to be afraid of anymore."

Then there is this beeping noise . . . and it won't stop beeping. . . .

I sit up in bed, and I realize that the beeping sound is coming from my beeper on the nightstand. I reach over and flash the light on the beeper screen. I see the 411 code after Bubbles's number. That's our secret signal. It means that Bubbles has something to tell me.

Sometimes Bubbles does that just to bother me. I mean, I'll get on the Internet to talk to her in the Phat Planet chat room, and she'll start talking about things that are *muy idiota*! You never know with Bubbles.

I look over at my clock, and I see that it is midnight. Quietly, I get up and go to my computer, and log on to the chat room to see what Bubbles wants.

I shake my head and rub my eyes. *Qué fantasía*. What a dream that was! Maybe I'd better carry an umbrella to school tomorrow, because after a dream like that, I know it's going to rain.

"We're in the house with the Mouse!" Bubbles types on the screen.

"Shouldn't Mickey be sleeping with Toto?" I type back. I'm going to get Bubbles good for this. Getting me out of bed for another one of her little jokes, *qué bromacita!* I'll bet you she's trying to tell me that the twins found another mouse in their closet—or maybe it's something to do with Abala Shaballa, that troublemaking witch.

"Not unless Toto is going to cut a *demo* with us, baby!!!" Bubbles types on the screen in response.

What is Bubbles talking about? I'm not in the mood for jokes. "Toto needs to be checking to see if you aren't going cuckoo," I type back, yawning.

"*Mouse Almighty* is the name of the producer Def Duck Records is hooking us up with—to cut a demo!" Bubbles types back.

Suddenly I'm wide awake. "What happened?" I type excitedly.

"That's right, *mamacita*. They're gonna let us cut a few songs for a possible demo tape!"

"*Ay, Dios mío*—my goodness—Bubbles, why didn't you just say so?!" I type, gasping now for air. "Does that mean we got a record deal?"

"No, but it means they're willing to spend

some development money to put us in the studio, and see what kind of chops we've got! We have to meet Mouse Almighty and Freddy Fudge—the A & R executive from Def Duck—at the record label office on Friday at four o'clock. What do you think about *that, mamacita*?!"

"I can't believe this is true!" I type on the screen. Then I tell Bubbles all about Princess Pamela's prediction—and about the dream I had.

"It's definitely gonna start raining Benjamins now, *mamacita!*" Bubbles replies.

"'It's Raining Benjamins.' That would make a great song title, no, Bubbles?" I type excitedly.

"That is so dope, Chuchie! I'm gonna start writing it right now! Powder to the People!"

I sign off, too, and drop back down on the bed, smiling happily. And then I start thinking. . . .

"Why does *Bubbles* always have to write the songs?" I ask myself. "How come she never lets *me* help write them? *I* wanna write the song 'It's Raining Benjamins.' After all, it was *my* idea. I'm going to tell Bubbles, that's what I'm gonna do."

I start getting so nervous about talking to

The Cheetah Girls

Bubbles—because I already know that we are going to fight. Tomorrow night, we're all going to the Times Square Tabernacle Church to see Derek in the "Mad Millennium" Fashion Show. (Bubbles agreed to go, to make up for what happened with the chokers. And then she made us all promise to come with her for support!)

I'll tell her then, I promise myself. On the other hand, maybe I *shouldn't* tell her. . . . Well, I'm sure not gonna tell her at school.

I toss and turn, praying that I have another dream, and float away on a magical umbrella. But nothing like that happens. Why did I have to come up with that song idea, anyway? Now I can't even be happy about the demo, because I'm so busy being upset—me with my *boca grande!*

Chapter 7

The next day at six o'clock, the five of us meet at Times Square Tabernacle Church on West Forty-third Street, to go see Derek Ulysses Hambone in the "Mad Millennium" Fashion Show.

Madrina gave us the money to pay for our tickets because she feels so bad about our "boo-boo" chokers venture. Once again, we're wearing our Cheetah Girls chokers—but, as Bubbles jokes, "Let's pray we don't drop alphabets in the good house of the Lord!"

We're all in a good mood, because of the great news about Def Duck Records. Even me. I'm still kinda nervous about talking to Bubbles about writing a new song with her. But I made a promise to myself last night, when I was lying awake in bed, that I am not going to do *el pollito*, and chicken out. I swear I'm going to pounce at the right moment!

I haven't even spoken to Dorinda about this, since she just automatically sides with Bubbles when it comes to things about the group. That's because she thinks Bubbles knows every-thing—which she doesn't!

Tonight, the twins especially are in seventh heaven about the news. But for a moment at least, when I first see them, my new hairdo dis-tracts them.

"Hey, Miss Chanel," Aqua exclaims. "Your hair looks *real* nice! Can I touch it? Ain't her hair pretty, Angie?"

"It sure is. It's so *looong*, Chanel!" Angie says, surprised.

"What did you think, I was wearing a weave under my braids or something?" I tease the twins.

"No, but I guess we didn't realize how *looooong* your hair really is."

As soon as she's through checking out my new 'do, Aqua tries to milk Bubbles for every *poco* detail about the phone call between Def

Duck Records and *Madrina*. "What did they say about us?"

"They said we wuz off the hook, Snook!" Bubbles says. (She loves being the one to tell us everything.) Aqua waits for more details, but Bubbles just looks at her and says, "That's it, really. They thought the showcase went really well, and now they want to put us in the studio to cut a demo—with a producer named Mouse Almighty. They said we should record three to five songs. Then they'll decide if they want to give us a record deal."

"Who is this Mouse Almighty?" Angie asks.

"They told Mom he's worked with a few other girl groups, so that's why they picked him to work with us. Let's see . . . he's worked with Karma's Children, the Lollipops, the Honey Dews, and In the Dark."

"In the Dark—who's that?" Dorinda wonders.

"You know—that little girl with the rhinestone-studded black eye patch, and the three other girls who prance around on stage with those monkey-head walking sticks, like they're all that," Aqua blurts out. "They went on tour once with Jiggie Jim and the Moonpies. Um, what's that song—oh . . . oh . . . 'Struck with Your Love and Now I See!' That's it!"

"Oh, them. I don't like them," Angie says, making a face.

"Well, the other groups he's worked with are dope, right?" Dorinda points out. "*And* he's got his own recording studio. That means he's got mad skills."

"Are we going to be able to record *your* songs?" I ask Bubbles.

"I don't know, Chuchie," Bubbles says, kinda humble. Then she breaks out a fresh wad of bubble gum. "He's the producer, so I guess we've gotta do whatever he tells us—'cuz Def Duck Records is paying for everything."

"Oh," I say. I can't get the nerve up to say anything about writing with Bubbles. Besides, I guess this isn't the right time. I don't want to talk about it in front of everybody.

"I'm telling y'all, this is the one," Aqua says, looking all satisfied with herself. "This is what we've been waiting for! I'm telling you, I know—because me and Angie have prayed enough about it!"

We go inside the church. Well, it's not exactly a church. It's more of an auditorium where they hold services. But I guess the twins are really happy just to be in *any* kind of church. They *love* going to church, and singing in the junior choir and everything.

Lady ushers with white gloves are standing at the entrance of the auditorium. "Good evening, sisters," Aqua and Angie greet them, all bubbly with excitement.

The ushers take our tickets and tear them in half. "Just go on inside and take a seat wherever you like, girls," they tell us.

"I hope the money is going to a good cause," heckles Bubbles as we go inside.

Dorinda has been reading the program intensively. Now she blurts out, "It says here, all the proceeds are going to the New York City Chapter for Homeless Women."

"That's good. That's real good," Aqua says, nodding her head in approval. (Their dad was the one who forked over the twenty dollars to pay for their two tickets, and I guess they feel better knowing it's all for a good cause.) Still, some things are more important than others, especially to the twins. "I hope they have good food here," Angie says, looking around.

"Amen to that," Aqua agrees. The only thing

the twins love more than going to church or singing is *eating*.

"They do have food—*afterward*," Bubbles tells them, rolling her eyes at the twins' incredible appetite.

A look of relief washes over Angie's face. "I've never been to a church service in an auditorium. What kind of church is this?" she asks us.

"I believe it's a 'nondenominational' church, but you know how they roll in New York. We can't have big, fancy churches like they have down South," Bubbles says, shrugging her shoulders.

(I'll bet church services in Houston must be in big, beautiful churches, *está bien?*)

"Look—it says here that the clothes are designed by students at Fashion Institute of Technology," Dorinda says, pointing to the program again.

"Oh, I get it. 'Up-and-coming' designers," Aqua volunteers.

"Yeah, let's just hope they have somewhere to '*go*' if their clothes are wack," Dorinda says with a chuckle.

"I wonder if Derek is here yet?" Bubbles asks, looking around for him.

Well, looky, cooky. Now that Derek is acting so mean to Bubbles, I think she kinda *likes* him. I'm not kidding. I know "goo-goo" eyes when I see them!

We take our seats, and wait for the fashion show to begin. Bubbles whips out her Kitty Kat notebook, and gets busy doing more work on her latest song, "Woof, There It Is!"

I try not to look, and luckily, the fashion show commentator comes on the stage. It's none other than Miss Clucky, the famous gossip columnist from television!

"Good evening, everyone. I'm Miss Clucky, and feeling lucky to be here with all of you! We're here to raise some money, and have some *fun!*"

Looking around at the audience, she lets out a big sigh. "Mmmm. Mmmm. I see we have some *fine*-looking young things in the audience tonight! You look *gooood*, y'all," she moans. Then she starts prancing back and forth in her red sequined gown, twirling to show off the draping cape thing attached to it. "*I* look *gooood*, too—don't I, y'all? Don't be shy, you can tell me!"

"*Yeah!*" the audience shouts in unison.

Personally, I think she looks like one of the ladies on the Goya float in the Dominican Day Parade—like she's full of beans!

"Hallelujah!" somebody shouts out.

Suddenly, *la lucha grande*—the big light-bulb—goes off in my head. That's it! *Hallelujah!* I can put it in the chorus of my first song—"It's raining Benjamins . . . *Hallelujah!* It's raining Benjamins . . . *Hallelujah!*"

I get so excited that I almost reach over to tell Bubbles, but Miss Clucky is still talking, so I keep my *boca* shut.

"Well, let's give some praise to fashion tonight, y'all!" Miss Clucky says, then puts on some funny-looking spectacles and begins to read from the index cards she has in her hands.

The show begins, and the models start coming out on stage to the beat of the music. Miss Clucky describes all the clothes they're wearing—some of which are definitely wack, but a few of which are definitely *la dopa!*

When Derek comes out on the stage modeling clothes, I poke Bubbles. "He looks gooood!" I whisper, imitating Miss Clucky.

We're sitting too far in the back of the audi-

torium for Derek to see us, but we wave anyway, giggling our heads off. Derek is wearing
this zebra-looking, long, flowing caftan, that
kinda looks like the clothes *Madrina* designs for
Toto in New York.

"That woulda looked more dope with one of
our chokers," Bubbles whispers to me. I can see
she feels bad, like we missed out on something.

After the fashion show, we head downstairs to
eat the buffet dinner. Dorinda is really excited
about all the clothes we saw, and she starts babbling about the outfits she's gonna design for
our shows when we go on tour to promote our
first album.

Bubbles stops her with a sharp comment. "If
you ask me, those designers tonight could definitely have used some Cheetah Girl flava."

Dorinda eyes the spread, and smirks. "Now,
that's what I'm talking about!"

We crowd around the buffet table, and put
heaps of potato salad, corn on the cob, fried
chicken, and baked beans on our plates. The
church ladies serving us say chirpily, "Aren't
y'all the cutest girls!"

"We're the Cheetah Girls," Dorinda says proudly.

"Mabel, look at those necklaces they got around their necks."

"Oh, these are our Cheetah Girl chokers," Bubbles pipes up, taking over the conversation. I'm surprised she doesn't tell them that we're selling them, so I turn to her and whisper, "Are we still selling the chokers?"

"To anybody with a ducket in a bucket!"

Right then, Derek Hambone comes over with his boy, Mackerel Johnson, and another tall, skinny guy we don't know. Now that the fashion show is over, Derek is back in his "street uniform"—a navy blue and red windbreaker with matching sweatpants.

He likes clothes from this designer, Johnny BeDown—a lot of the kids in our school wear his stuff, but *we* think it's ticky-tacky because it has too many letters on it. Like Bubbles says, "Why should we wear clothes with anybody else's name on it but our own?"

"Hey, Cheetah Girls! Glad to see you in the house," Derek says. Then he reaches over and kisses Bubbles on the cheek! I can't believe she let him do that!

"We figured out how to make the chokers," Bubbles blurts out, fingering the one around her neck. "We've already taken orders for five more."

"That's cool," Derek says, kinda laughing. "It's all good in the 'hood."

What does Bubbles mean, she's taken orders for five more chokers? She didn't tell *me* anything! *Nada. Vampira*-tooth Mackerel winks at me. I guess I'd better be *super-simpática* too to make up for what happened. "What program are you in?" I ask Mackerel, even though it kills me. I feel my face turning *rosa*.

"Design," he mumbles. His voice is so soft, I can hardly hear it.

"Did you like the clothes in the show?" I ask, trying to seem like I'm interested in talking with him. I guess it's okay—as long as he doesn't start biting my neck!

"They *awwriight,* but I'm trying to flow with the street vibe," he continues—like he's flossing about his design skills.

"Whose clothes do you like?"

"I dig Trace Gear, you know what I'm saying?"

"Oh, I like that, too," I say, telling a *poco* fiberoni. I hate their clothes, because they're too baggy—but I'm not going to tell *him* that, *está bien?*

"You know what? I'll buy another choker from you, if you're still selling them," Mackerel says. Then he *winks* at me. *Cuatro yuks*—he's *flirting* with me!

If he would just keep his "trap" shut, so I wouldn't have to look at his teeth, maybe I wouldn't mind. Those teeth of his give me "the spookies." He ought to get them fixed, you know?

"Okay, *está bien*," I say to Mackerel. Then I pull on Bubbles's sleeve and ask her what to do.

"That's cool—we've got enough chokers. We can handle it," Bubbles says confidently. "That is, if it's okay with you, Derek?"

Bubbles is trying to be sooo charming to Derek—and he is eating it up like, well, a Red Snapper!

"It's cool with Mr. DUH—you know what I'm saying?"

Bubbles blushes deep purple. See, Derek has the initials of his first, middle, and last name shaved on the back of his head. That's how they roll in Detroit, where he comes from—but we think that look is so played. Besides, with initials like his, he shouldn't be broadcasting them, *está bien*? That's why we always make fun of him. But *la gente* at school obviously told him about *that* nickname, too.

"You know . . . I'm sorry about what happened," Bubbles says, and she seems like she means it for a change!

"Yeah, I know, Cheetah Girl," Derek says, grinning and showing off his gold front tooth. "Does that mean you'll go out with me, yo?"

I want to scream. *Ay, caramba!* Bubbles, *please* say *no!*

"All right. We can move, we can groove," Bubbles responds.

I think I'm going to faint! Dorinda's mouth is hanging open, too. I look over my shoulder, and see that the twins are busy talking to Derek's friend, whom we don't know.

"Bubbles, we have to go," I blurt out.

"Hold up, Miss *Señorita*, I'm trying to make things happen, you know what I'm saying?" Derek says, interrupting me.

"*Sí*," I say nastily, like, "DUH! I can see that."

"I'll check you tomorrow," Derek says to Bubbles. "Make me another choker, too. *Ayiight?*"

"Bet," Bubbles says, as Derek and Mackerel move off to work the room.

Galleria, Dorinda, and I make our way to one of the banquet tables, and sit down with our food.

"Bubbles, are you really going to go out with Derek?" Dorinda asks amused.

"No, silly-willy! I'm just trying to make up for what happened," Bubbles says, exasperated. "And you'll notice I got our choker enterprise back in business, too—we've got new orders from both Derek and Mackerel. By the way, who was that guy they were with? Does he look familiar?"

"*Tales from the Crypt,* maybe?" I retort. Now I wanna ask Bubbles about those orders for five chokers she told Derek we had. "How come you didn't tell me we got orders for five chokers?" I ask defensively.

"'Cuz we *don't* have orders for five chokers, Chuchie. Use that *cabeza* of yours for a change and some coins," Bubbles huffs, knocking on my head with her knuckles. "I just said that to Derek, the *gnocco*, to drum up some business."

"What's a *gnocco*?" I ask, annoyed.

"A blockhead," Bubbles says mischievously. Here she just got in trouble for calling Derek names, and already she has a new one for him? That's Bubbles—always in trouble.

As for me, I don't care what she says—I *do* use my *cabeza*—because I'm not the one getting all cuckoo over some *blockhead* with a gold mine in his mouth!

The twins stop talking with Derek's friend and come over to join us at our table. "One of the ushers asked me if she could buy two of our chokers for her daughters—they're twins, like us," Aqua says excitedly, then pulls out a piece of paper with a name and phone number on it.

"We could sell two to her *right now*—because we have the five that we remade," Bubbles points out.

"I'll be right back with the cash," Aqua says, grabbing the chokers from Bubbles and jumping up to find the usher.

We sit there, not saying a word. As for me, I'm still fuming at Galleria for knocking on my head with her knuckles.

Then Angie pipes up. "His name is Spider, by the way—and he is a member of this church."

"Who?" Dorinda asks, puzzled.

"Derek's friend. He goes to DeWitt Clinton High School in the Bronx."

"Look at Angie, trying to make moves!" Bubbles says proudly. "Houston's in the house!"

"Well, I was just trying to be nice, since Derek is the one who invited y'all," Angie says, kinda embarrassed. (The twins never talk about boys.) "You know our daddy would ship us back to Granddaddy Walker's Funeral Home in little pieces if he ever even *thought* we were going out with boys!"

"How gruesome," Bubbles chuckles.

"I'm saving myself for Krusher," I coo.

"You couldn't even win a contest for a date with him, Chuchie. How are you gonna go out with him?" Bubbles asks, rolling her eyes at me.

I'm going to kill Bubbles! Luckily at that moment, Aqua runs back to the table, holding twenty dollars in her hand.

Then she sees that Bubbles is frowning. "We *are* selling them for ten dollars each, right?" Aqua asks puzzled.

"Yeah," Bubbles says absentmindedly. She is obviously thinking about something else entirely. "Oh, yeah . . . I'll hang on to the money till we split it up."

That's *it*! I'm so mad at her, I'm not even

scared anymore to ask her about the song. "Bubbles, can I write 'It's Raining Benjamins' with you?"

"What?" Bubbles looks like she's been hit by a truck.

Dorinda looks at me, smiling nervously. She knows exactly what's going to happen—Bubbles and I are about to have a big fight!

Even Aqua stops babbling for a change.

Poking her mouth out, Bubbles says in a really annoyed tone, "Chuchie, you couldn't even figure out how to glue letters on the Cheetah Girl chokers. Now you're gonna try to write songs, too? *Please*—don't make me sneeze."

"Here's a Kleenex," I say nastily, whipping a package of tissues out of my backpack. "I'll bet you I can write songs just as well as you can!"

"You two need to *stop*!" Dorinda says, jumping in before Bubbles and I start pulling each other's hair out. She has seen us fight before, so she knows. *Ella sabe, está bien?*

"Chuchie, I just don't think it's a good idea for you to write the songs with me," Bubbles says, like she is Judge Jonas on television and she's got a gavel to pound.

"Then I'm *leaving*!" I shout, wincing because leaving the Cheetah Girls is the last thing I want to do.

"Don't do that, Chanel!" Dorinda says, trying to reason with me.

"No, I'm sick of Bubbles trying to run everything!" I say. I can feel the tears welling up in my eyes, but I'm not gonna let her see me cry. I turn to go.

"Come on, y'all, let's *all* go," Aqua says, pushing her plate aside and getting to her feet.

We all walk outside in silence, and head to the subway station. I'm the only one going downtown, so I take the train by myself.

Dorinda runs after me on the platform and gives me a hug. "Don't worry, Chanel. I'm gonna talk to Galleria. This isn't right, that the two of you are always fighting."

"Whatever," I say quietly, then hug Dorinda back. Bubbles doesn't even say good-bye to me, and I act like I don't care. If she wants to control everything so badly, then let her! She can run the whole jiggy jungle by herself, for all I care!

Chapter 8

The next morning before school, Bubbles calls me on my bedroom phone.

"Look, Chuchie. If you want to *try* to write a song with me, then we can do it at your house before we have rehearsal later."

"Okay," I say like I don't care. "Whatever." Maybe Bubbles is pulling one of her tricks.

"Chuchie, I *said* we'll try to write a song together. What more do you want me to say?"

"*Nada. Pero* you could apologize for embarrassing me in front of *everybody*." I realize I am screaming into the receiver; that I'm being "emotional"—just like Mom.

"Okay, calm down, *Señorita*. I'm sorry,

okay?" Bubbles huffs. "Take a chill pill, *pleez.*"

Now I feel so embarrassed for acting cuckoo that I just say, "Okay, I'll see you later." I quickly hang up the receiver, then stick my tongue out at it. That's what Bubbles does—cause trouble—just because she always wants everybody to do what *she* wants!

We should be happy that Def Duck Records is letting us record some songs for a demo tape, but instead, all I feel is worried that Bubbles is going to try to boss us around!

By the time I meet up with Dorinda and Bubbles at school, I see we're back in the Cheetah Girls choker business.

"Look! I already got the twenty dollars from Derek and Mackerel," Bubbles says, jumping up and down. "We've got forty dollars now—and counting. Here, you two try to sell two each," Bubbles commands me and Dorinda, handing us each a pair of chokers.

"Bet," says Dorinda. She gives me a hug and smiles. I realize that Bubbles probably already told her that we talked on the phone this morning. Sometimes, Dorinda and I talk on the phone, too—without Bubbles—because I think of Dorinda as a sister now. But *not* a sister that I sometimes *hate*—like Bubbles!

"You know, we should figure out how much exactly it costs us to make the chokers, so we make sure to charge enough," Dorinda says, all businesslike.

Bubbles is right. Dorinda does have her eye on the ka-*ching*—the cash register. It's really true!

Bubbles gives Dorinda a look, like, "Hold up—*I'm* running this choker show," which makes Dorinda squirm a little.

"I mean, we should write down all the money we spend for materials, um, just to make sure," Do' Re Mi says sheepishly.

"Yeah—you're right, we'll do that later," Galleria says, brushing her off. "For now, let's just roll with the duckets coming in the bucket!" Bubbles has taken command again.

We do the Cheetah Girls handshake together—but inside, I don't feel okay about everything. I don't think Bubbles is serious about letting me write a song with her after school today. She just said that to get off the hook.

"Just a reminder, we have to meet Mouse

Almighty and Freddy Fudge at the Def Duck Record Company office on Friday at four." Bubbles is talking like *she's* our manager now.

"Are we gonna record?" Dorinda asks.

"Not this time," Galleria tells her. "We're just meeting with the producer, so he can get to know us, and check out our vibe. The way the record company executive explained it, we're just going there for a 'meet and greet.' After Mouse gets a feel for our flavor, he goes out and shops around for songs he thinks are right for us. Then he puts us in a studio to record them, and cut a mini demo tape."

"Word!" Dorinda says, squinting her eyes. You can tell she's really interested in how everything works.

"Where do we have to go?" I ask.

"They have a New York office at Thirty Rock."

"*Where?*" I ask again, annoyed. I mean, we're not going mountain climbing, *está bien?*

"Thirty Rockefeller Plaza, Chuchie—right by the ice skating rink where we used to go, back in the junior high school days."

"Okay, Bubbles—I didn't understand what you were saying," I hiss at her.

It's Raining Benjamins

Dorinda looks at us like, "Don't you two start again!"

Today, my last class of the day is Italian, which I don't really like at all. See, it's kinda hard, and I'm not that good with languages—except for Spanish and English. Two is enough, *está bien?* I'm only taking Italian because Bubbles made me do it. I wanted to take Spanish, but she got really upset with me.

"Chuchie, you *are* Spanish," she protested—which made me feel guilty, because it is *la verdad*. But why shouldn't I take a class that's easy for a change—*para un cambio?* It's not like Bubbles is helping me with my homework—even though I haven't asked her. But then again, why *should* I have to ask? She should *know* I need help!

I'm not listening to my teacher, Mr. Lepidotteri, because I'm too busy trying to write the words to "It's Raining Benjamins." It makes me feel so cool—*tan coolio*—that I am writing a song. Okay—*trying* to write a song.

Now I'm frustrated, though. I wanted to have the whole song written by lunchtime, so I could show Bubbles that I really can do it. Instead, I have simply scribbled, *"Ayúdame!—*

help me!"—all over the margins, with unsmiley faces all around the border.

Luiza Santiago, my classmate, glances over and sees my doodles. When the class is over, I make a big deal of sighing—like I'm so relieved, and have better things to do with my time, *está bien?* Luiza leans over and studies my scribbles, then asks curiously, "What does '*ayú-dame*' mean?"

Luiza is "Spanglish," like me—mostly Nuyorican, which means she is Puerto Rican born in Nueva York—and part Chilean.

Unlike me, Luiza doesn't speak a word of Spanish.

"It means 'help me,'" I say, giggling. "I'm trying to write this song 'It's Raining Benjamins' for my group—but I guess the only thing I've figured out is where the doodles go!"

I can tell that Luiza is impressed, because she keeps staring at the doodled page, and tries to decipher more of my scribbles. "It must be kinda hard, writing a song."

"Yeah. I mean I've got the general idea, but it just takes a lot of time to get it down on paper. You know how I am—I can't sit still," I say apologetically.

Luiza tries to figure out some of the words on the page, and reads them aloud. "'There's precipatation in the nation . . . and not the kind you think—'"

Interrupting Luiza, I blurt out, "I think I've misspelled 'precipatation.'"

"I think it's p-r-e-c-i-p-i-t-a-t-i-o-n," Luiza says slowly. "I think that's right. Yeah, that's right."

I hurriedly cross out the "a," and replace it with an "i." That's all I need, is for Bubbles to see that I misspell words. She'll be like, "See, I told you, Chuchie, you can't write a song!"

So what if I'm not as good at spelling as Bubbles? When we were in grade school, she always won the spelling bees. In the sixth grade, she even made it to the nationals of the spelling bee contests. Me, I'm lucky if I can spell my own name. But that doesn't mean I can't write songs, does it?

As *la gente* start leaving the classroom, I suddenly realize that I didn't hear the homework assignment.

"Luiza!" I yell after her. "What's the homework?"

She just shakes her head at me, and opens

her notebook. "Idioms that go with the verb *avere*."

Idioms? I feel like an *idiota*, because I don't know what that means. "What's an idiom?" I ask.

Now Luiza is getting a little annoyed. "Here," she says, thrusting the notebook in my hand, and letting me read the homework assignment for myself.

"Oh, I get it," I say, feeling like a *babosa*.

After I leave class, I take a deep breath and get ready for Freddy. The twins taught us this expression, and I don't know exactly what it means. I think in this case, it means "I'm ready for bigmouthed Bubbles!"

Bubbles comes over to my house an hour earlier than the rest of the Cheetah Girls, so that we can write the song together. Dorinda has gone to the library to study, so she won't have to go all the way home, then all the way back downtown again for rehearsal.

"Hey, Pucci, wazzup?" Bubbles exclaims.

Pucci *loves* Bubbles, and is always trying to show her his latest trading cards, stuffed animals, or whatever new computer gadget he's got in his room. Sometimes he tells her jokes, too.

"Bubbles, what did the elephant say to the alligator after he swallowed him?" Pucci says, grinning at her like she's the cat's meow.

"Um, lemme see—'Don't chomp on my intestines, 'cuz that's my lunch, you scaly toad'?"

"No!" Pucci says, almost giggling himself to death before he gets the joke out. "He said, 'Poop you later, alligator'! Heeheeheeheehee!!!"

"That's disgusting, Pucci!" I sneer, growling so Pucci knows I don't think his jokes are *funny*.

Bubbles, of course, giggles at Pucci's joke, like he's Dr. Doolittle or something.

"Bubbles, you coming to my birthday on Saturday?" Pucci asks her wistfully.

"Um, of course, Pucci. You're the man!" I notice her looking at me when she says it, like it doesn't matter if I want her there, because now Pucci invited her.

"Come on, let's go in the living room." I motion to Bubbles. Having Pucci around is cramping my style.

Galleria plops her Kitty Kat notebook down on the table, then whispers, "What are you gonna do about getting him a pet for his birth-day?"

"*Nada*," I whine.

"What are you gonna get him?"

"*Nada*," I repeat.

"You have to get him *something*, Chuchie," Bubbles snaps.

"No, I don't."

"I'm not fighting with you about it," Bubbles says. Then she whips open her notebook, and starts acting like she's a *real* songwriter. "Chuchie, you're gonna see. It's not so easy to write a song, 'cuz the inspiration has to hit you. Then it just kinda comes out."

"I know that," I reply.

"Well, lemme see what you got so far."

As I take out my school notebook from my backpack and put it on the table, I sheepishly tell her the truth. "I don't really have much. I, um, just thought it would be fun if we did it together."

"I know, Chuchie—but you must have written down something!" Bubbles says, kinda annoyed.

"Yeah," I say, hesitating. I open the Italian section of my notebook, and shove the page in her face.

"W-what is *this?*" she asks, stammering. "Doodle hour?"

"No, look! What about this?" I say, pointing to the one line I wrote on the page.

Bubbles reads it aloud. "'There's precipitation in the nation, and not the kind you think— stop blinking, and don't pass me those shades . . . .' That's good . . . we could definitely work with that. . . ."

Bubbles takes a deep breath, like she's going to give me a lecture, then taps her pencil on the table. "Chuchie, first you have to write *verses* for the song, okay?"

What's a verse? I wonder. But I say, "Yeah, I know that, Bubbles."

"So. Let's work on the first verse," she says, flipping to a page in her Kitty Kat notebook. The page is filled with lots of scribbling. Obviously, she has already been working a lot on the song.

"Look at this," Bubbles says, pointing to a line on the page.

I read aloud what Bubbles has written, "'Dollar bills sure give me thrills, but it's nothing like the Benjamins, baby. Don't maybe, awrighty, they're mighty.'"

Without thinking, I blurt out my reaction. "It

kinda sounds like the song those girls, CMG, were singing in the New Talent Showcase."

"Yeah? So?" Bubbles retorts. "It's not *exactly* the same. You can't say that I'm *copying* them, 'cuz here's *their* song."

Bubbles turns to another page in her notebook, and reads aloud. "'Yeah, we roll with Lincoln/What are you thinkin'?'" Bubbles frowns. "That's kinda like what *you* wrote, Chuchie," she points out. "So don't go accusing *me* of copying!"

"Well, I don't know. We *both* wrote things that kinda sound like theirs," I volunteer. "'Thinking. Awrighty. Mighty.' It sounds the same, right?"

"Okay, scratch that," Bubbles humphs, kinda annoyed. "Let's start again."

"Oh! Oh!" I say, getting all excited. "I thought of something to put at the end!"

"What?" Bubbles asks, like she's not sure she wants to hear it.

"'It's raining Benjamins . . . Hallelujah! It's raining Benjamins . . . . Hallelujah!'"

"Hmmm . . . instead of 'Hallelujah,' how about this—' for a change and some coins . . . It's raining Benjamins . . . I heard that'?"

"That's even better!" I tell her.

It's Raining Benjamins

"Okay—now that part's called the chorus," Bubbles says. "That's where the group sings the same thing together."

"Chorus," I repeat. "Okay."

Bubbles's wheels are spinning a mile a minute. "I like that . . . that'll work. . . ." All of a sudden, she is deep in thought, scribbling madly.

I don't want to disturb her. I've seen her do this a million times, and the songs always come out *la dopa*.

"How about we start it with—'For the first time in *her*-story/There's a weather forecast that looks like cash . . .'"

"I like that!" I say, getting into the groove. "Then, how about something like, 'Put on your shoes and spread the news'?"

"Yeah!" Bubbles says. "That'll work!" Writing some more, she says, "Okay—'So tie your shoes to spread the news/And come around the bend at half past ten!'"

For the next hour, Bubbles and I go back and forth like this, until we have two verses and the chorus. Bubbles starts humming a melody to go with the words.

"You really are better at that than I am," I

admit to her. "How do you come up with the beat?"

"I don't know, Chuchie. It just comes to me, I guess," Bubbles says, shrugging her shoulders and smiling sweetly. "Sometimes I start hearing the melody of a song before I even think of the words."

"Oh!" I say with surprise. "Well, I guess I'm not really a songwriter—but I do want to help sometimes, okay?"

"Well . . ." Bubbles says, hesitating, "I guess so—but I don't feel right giving you equal credit."

"*Credit?*" I ask in surprise, because I'm not sure what she's talking about.

"You know—*songwriting* credit, in case the song ever gets published or something." Bubbles is acting like she knows everything about the music business, *está bien?*

I can't believe her. She can be so selfish about some things! *Yo no entiendo*—I don't understand why she does that. I love her, and would do anything for her—and she *knows* that. *Why doesn't she do the same thing for me?*

Then, all of a sudden, the strength of all the *brujas* who traveled the earth on broomsticks gives me the courage to speak up for myself. I blurt out, "Bubbles, if you don't give me song-writing credit, I'm never gonna speak to you again!"

"Okay, you *gnocca!*" Bubbles blurts back at me, beaten for once in her life. Then a sly grin spreads over her face, as she gets her usual last word in. "But only if it gets published, you understand?"

"*Yo entiendo perfectamente*, I understand per-fectly, you *babosa*," I hiss at her—which sends Bubbles into a fit of giggles.

By the time the twins and then Dorinda arrive, Bubbles and I are still giggling about our first songwriting experience. I start dancing around the living room, singing "'It's raining Benjamins . . . for a change and some coins . . . It's raining Benjamins . . . I heard that . . . It's r-a-i-n-i-n-g . . . again!'"

Chapter 9

If I thought staying at the Royal Rooster Hotel on Hollywood Boulevard was something to cluck about, the Def Duck Records office in Rockefeller Plaza has definitely laid the golden egg!

"How tall do you think that thing is?" I mumble to Dorinda, as we both gaze in awe at the gold duck statue in the lobby.

"About fifty feet," Dorinda says, eyeing the duck statue like it's gonna start quacking. "They musta had a lot of artists with gold records to lay this thing!"

"Elevator is that way, ladies," says the security guard in the lobby, pointing to the back.

"Look, *that* elevator goes to the ninety-second

floor!" Bubbles whispers to me, because she doesn't want the twins to hear her. They are bigger scaredy-cats than the scarecrow in the *Wizard of Oz* when it comes to riding elevators.

Madrina pushes the button for the forty-ninth floor, and I'm just hoping the twins don't have a barf attack in front of the record company executives!

"I guess we can't ask the record company to move their offices to a lower floor *yet*," *Madrina* says, putting her arm around Aquanette. "Not until they give us a deal, huh?"

"No, ma'am," Aqua says. She always gets very formal when she's scared.

Gracias, gooseness, I think, as we step into the reception area. The twins held on to their lunch.

The reception area is really quiet. I thought there would be music playing everywhere. Mr. Freddy Fudge comes to get us. He's a tall, skinny guy with blond, short, fuzzy hair, and a chocolate-brown complexion like the twins. He looks *tan coolio*, too, in his black-and-white-checked blazer with a red handkerchief in the pocket. I almost blurt out that red is one of my favorite colors, but I'm too nervous to even speak!

"We met an A & R gentlemen, Mr. Tom Isaaks, at the New Talent Showcase in Los Angeles," *Madrina* tells Freddie Fudge as we walk down the hallway.

"Yes, he's on the West Coast." Mr. Fudge then goes on to explain that he too is an A&R development executive——*for R&B artists.*

We're not R&B artists! I think to myself—but I'm not saying anything. Bubbles looks at me and raises her eyebrows.

Luckily, *Madrina* says something before Bubbles does." Mr. Fudge——"

"Call me Freddy," he says, as we walk down a long, skinny hallway past a whole lot of cubicles and offices. Everybody seems really busy here.

"Freddy—you know, the Cheetah Girls aren't really an R & B group."

"Oh, I know, Mrs. Garibaldi," Freddy says apologetically. "It's just a catchphrase in the music business, for, um, 'urban music.'"

"Oh. Okay," *Madrina* says, smiling. "The girls like to think of their music as 'global groove.'"

"Excellent. There's a hook we can really work with—that is, if everything works out,"

Freddy says cautiously. He opens the door to a conference room, and motions for us to step inside.

"Thank you—" I say, then stop myself from saying his name, because I'm not sure if it's okay for *us* to call him Freddy, or if we're supposed to call him Mr. Fudge. I'll ask *Madrina* later.

Mr. Fudge introduces us to the three other people sitting in the room. "This is my assistant, Haruko Yamahaki. Mouse Almighty, the producer you'll be working with for the next few months—and hopefully longer than that, if everything goes well—and Mr. Chunky Carter, one of our new talent coordinators."

After sitting down at the conference table, *Madrina* pipes up. "Freddy, you mentioned something about a test single—"

"Yes, Mrs. Garibaldi. Let me explain. Mouse is going to be responsible for selecting songs from various songwriters that he feels would really showcase the Cheetah Girls," Freddy says, his hands propped up on the table, folded in a tent position.

"If we feel that the songs are *strong* enough, the Cheetah Girls will be given a record deal option with Def Duck, for the release of one 'test single.' If that single tests well in the marketplace, the girls will then be given a full record deal, and you'll go back in the studio and cut an album."

"I see," Mrs. Garibaldi says.

"I know it's a long process," Mr. Fudge continues. "But these days, we only add a certain number of artists to our roster each year. That way, we can spend the proper time, energy, and money on artist development, marketing, and promotion. I hope you understand that."

"Yes, we do—although you'll soon see that these girls have *already* been groomed to take over the world!" *Madrina* says with a knowing chuckle.

Everybody in the conference room laughs along with her, including Haruko, who has a *funny* laugh. All of a sudden, I start to feel more relaxed. Looking around, I see that my crew is feeling the same way.

"Would you girls like a soda?" Haruko asks, her dark eyes twinkling. "Take one, please."

I can't stop staring at Haruko's lips. Her red lipstick looks really *la dopa* with her long black straight hair. I *love* red lipstick—even though I don't wear it yet, because I'm afraid I'll mess it up. I wonder how she gets it to look so *perfect*.

"We would love a soda," Aqua pipes up, which for some crazy reason gets us all giggling again.

Now Chunky starts talking, telling us that he will be working with us to coordinate our studio sessions with Mouse, and handling everything else that needs to be done.

"Why don't you girls tell us a little about yourselves?" Mouse suggests, then leans back into his chair like a Big Willy. He doesn't look like a Mouse at all. I wonder how he got his name. . . .

"Well," Bubbles says, speaking up for us. "We're wanna-be stars in the jiggy jungle, I guess."

Haruko does that laugh again, which makes me laugh, too. Bubbles looks at me, but I'm sorry—I can't help it.

"How did you girls hook up?" Chunky asks, curious.

"Chuchie, I mean, Chanel and I have been friends since we were born. See, our mothers used to be models together, and then my mom became Chanel's godmother and everything."

"Chanel and Galleria and I all go to the same high school—Fashion Industries East," Dorinda says, smiling and showing off her cute little dimples.

"And we met *them* at the Kats and Kittys Klub!" Aqua explains enthusiastically. "We wuz singing by the barbecue grill, and they just *loved* us!"

Now Bubbles and I start laughing loudly—because that's not exactly true. Aqua is telling a fib-eroni. Bubbles *hated* her and Angie at first, because she thought they were show-offs.

Actually, I think Bubbles was just kinda jealous, because we'd never been asked to sing at a Kats and Kittys party, and we're from New York. Then here come Angie and Aqua, straight out of Houston, and they just kinda take over, *está bien?*

After we blab some more about our music, Mr. Freddy Fudge is back down to business. "What I will need is for you and the girls to sign an agreement. It states that Def Duck is providing the financial arrangements for a demo tape, but we're under no obligation to give you a record deal until such time as we deem it viable to enter into such an agreement."

"I'll have my lawyer look it over, and get back to you," *Madrina* says, like a real manager.

"Okay," Mr. Fudge says, rising from the table and reaching over to shake *Madrina*'s hand.

We say good-bye to everyone fifty times. As we're leaving, Dorinda turns to Haruko and says, "Thank you for the soda. Um, I like your name."

Haruko laughs that funny laugh of hers again, and replies, "I like yours, too."

"What does yours mean?" Dorinda asks curiously, looking around at us to make sure she's not holding up anything.

"It means 'child born in the spring' in Japanese," Haruko says, beaming like she's really happy someone asked her something about herself. "What does yours mean, Dorinda?"

"'God's gift,'" Dorinda says, smiling back.

Madrina puts her arms around Dorinda and says, "Come on, 'God's gift.' Let's go eat a well-deserved early dinner."

We all wave good-bye to each other fifty more times, before we finally head back down to the lobby, where Mr. Golden Duck Statue is still standing.

Bubbles waves good-bye to the statue. "Good-bye, Mr. Ducky, you made us feel lucky!" she says.

"Hey! That's a song!" I exclaim, feeling like I'm sitting on top of the world.

"That's *not* a song, Chuchie," Bubbles says, giggling. But she's really nice about it, and puts her arm around me.

I guess she's right—that would be a stupid song. Still, I'm so excited about the fact that Bubbles and I wrote a song together that I tell *Madrina* all about it as we walk down the street.

"I like it!" *Madrina* says, when I tell her the words to the refrain. "God knows we could use a cash money shower right about now—even if it's only a shower of George Washingtons!"

Chapter 10

"**Y**ou know," *Madrina* says as we stand on the corner, waiting for the light to change, "if this all works out, I'm going to talk to the record company executives about recording some of *your* songs."

"That's a done deal-io!" Bubbles says excitedly.

"You know, at the end of the day in this business, it's all about publishing rights," *Madrina* says, getting serious. "That's where the real money falls from the sky."

"Publishing rights—what are they?" Dorinda asks.

"Well," *Madrina* explains, "the person who *writes* the song collects publishing royalties for as long as the song sells, is played on the radio, gets used for motion picture soundtracks or television commercials—you name it, there's a way to claim publishing payments."

"Word? That's dope!" Dorinda says. And now I can see that the songwriting wheels are turning in *her* head, too.

"Well, we've got to try to get every ducket in the bucket," Bubbles says emphatically. Then she turns to me. "Chuchie, we're gonna have to work on our song some more, you know?"

"*Yo sé, mamacita!*" I say enthusiastically.

"What time do we have to be at your house on Saturday?" she asks me.

"Noon, I guess," I say wistfully, because it suddenly hits me that I still don't have a present for Pucci. And now that the day is almost here, I realize that I can't just get him *nada*, like I said.

"*Madrina*, do you think I could have my paycheck today instead of Saturday?" I ask, in my sweetest voice.

For working three afternoons at Toto in New York . . . Fun in Diva Sizes, I get forty dollars a week—half of which I have to give to Mom to pay back the charges I sneaked on her credit card like a *babosa*.

"I think we can arrange something," *Madrina* says. "You're buying Pucci a birthday present?" she asks excitedly.

"Well, I guess," I say, kinda puzzled.

"Chuchie, here," Bubbles says, taking some money out of her cheetah wallet and stuffing it into my hand.

I must be dreaming, because Bubbles wouldn't give me money if the sky was falling.

"*Qué es esto?*" I ask Bubbles, my voice squeaking. "What's this?"

"It's the money from the chokers. You can have it, all right?" Bubbles turns to the twins and Dorinda for their approval.

"That's fine with us," Aqua pipes up. "I mean, come on, Chanel, you gotta give your brother more than a birthday card for his birthday! Ain't that right, Angie?"

"Yes, ma'am, that's right," Angie replies.

"Don't worry. We're gonna keep track of all the money, the way Mom does for the store," Bubbles says, pulling out a cheetah notebook out of a paper bag. "You can pay us back our share later—after you get done paying back your mother." She turns to Dorinda. "Do' Re Mi, why don't you keep the book on it?"

Dorinda's face lights up like a Christmas tree. "Word! I'll keep track of everything!"

"Good—'cuz quiet as it's kept, you're the brains behind the Cheetah Girls operation," Bubbles says proudly.

I can't believe how humble Galleria's being. That's not *like* her. *Es la verdad*—it's the truth!

"I'll go with you to buy Pucci a pet," Bubbles volunteers.

"What pet is that, darling?" *Madrina* asks, because she knows Mom does not like pets—unless it's a Chia Pet that just has to be watered!

"Chuchie's gonna buy Pucci a hog!" Bubbles says mischievously.

"Now, I *know* that must be some Cheetah Girls joke, because Juanita will ground Chanel for the rest of her life if it isn't!" *Madrina* says sternly.

"Bubbles doesn't mean a real hog, *Madrina*—it's an African pygmy hedgehog," I try to explain.

"Chanel, *that* sounds even worse—like some kind of animal used for a voodoo ritual or something!" *Madrina* says, looking alarmed. "Listen, Chanel, you two work this out over dinner, because I'm getting so hungry I may just eat a pygmy whatever-it-is!"

We all eat like we're starving for Marvin. After, *Madrina* says, "I'm heading home. I've got work to do. Galleria, I'll see you later. And don't bring back a pet with more growl power than you girls have." With a wave, she heads off toward the subway station.

"We'll come with y'all to the pet store if you want," Aqua volunteers.

I guess we're all in such a good mood because of the meeting—and the *lonchando*—that we don't want to leave each other just yet. After all, there'll be plenty of time for homework and headaches later.

"I can come, too," Do' Re Mi chimes in. And that settles it. We all take off down the street, singing "Shop in the Name of Love"—one of Galleria's tunes—at the top of our lungs.

The Exotica Pet Store on Tenth Avenue looks like a jungle paradise. Still, the snakes in the big glass case don't look like they're exactly having a ball. They seem like they're kinda cramped— and not too happy about it either.

"Too bad they don't have any dogs here," I

moan, looking around at all the exotic pets. I see a sign that says, WE'VE GOT REPTILES—NOT POODLES—SO DON'T ASK!

"Chuchie, Mom is right," Bubbles says firmly. "We'll be lucky if we can pull off this charade—giving Pucci a pet that fits in the palm of his hand."

"I'll tell you one thing," I shoot back. "We'd never get away with a dog!"

"Oooh, what kind of fish is that?" Dorinda asks, pressing her nose against the fish tank to ogle a bright-yellow fish with blue lips.

"Miss, don't lean on the fish tanks!" snaps a snarly salesman with wild curly red hair and big black glasses.

"Okay, Mr. Magoo," Dorinda mumbles under her breath, then, more loudly, asks again, "I just wanted to know what kind of fish this is—that's *all*."

"That's a blue-lipped angelfish, okay?"

Now I'm getting nervous, because Mr. Magoo is kinda mean.

"Bubbles, *you* ask him," I whisper. She's not afraid to stand up to grown-ups who are nasty and *antipático*.

"We want to see an African pygmy hedgehog, please," Bubbles says with authority.

Dorinda pulls my sleeve and says, "We gotta make sure it's a baby, though—because they only live to be six years old."

"Okay."

Meanwhile, Mr. Magoo is standing there, waiting for us to finish whispering. "You ready, or what?"

"Yes, sir. We want a baby one, okay?"

"Yeah, yeah. Everybody wants a baby. I don't know what I'm supposed to do with these animals when they're more than a day old," Mr. Magoo huffs, throwing us a dirty look. "They're over there in the cage by the wall. Next to the guinea pigs."

"Oh, that's good!" Aqua says, getting excited. The twins have two guinea pigs for pets—Porgy and Bess—and they're really cute.

"He is so mean, I don't know if we should buy a pet here. Maybe he abuses the animals," I say as we hightail it to the back of the store.

"Don't worry, the animals probably just ignore him and eat their carrots in peace," Bubbles replies. "It's not like they're dogs or cats, Chuchie."

"Ooh, *mira*, look!" I exclaim, when I see a

bunch of little brown creatures sitting in their cage, just staring up at us.

Mr. Magoo is right behind us and snarls, "Lemme open the cage, all right?" Next thing I know, he puts a hedgehog in my hand, warning, "The spines are very sharp—so don't go scaring him."

"Can we have a girl one?" Dorinda asks.

"No, Do'—it's for Pucci, not us," Bubbles reminds her.

"Oooh, look at how he's scratching my hand!" I coo. I love him already!

"What do they eat?" Angie asks.

"They like insects, frogs, mice," Mr. Magoo says in a huffy tone, like we're stupid or something.

"How much is it?" I ask nervously.

"Forty-two bucks."

I look at Bubbles, and my eyes are saying *ayúdame!* "I only have forty dollars."

"I'll put in the rest," Bubbles volunteers.

"Is that it?" Mr. Magoo asks.

"Yes, sir!" I say excitedly.

Wait till Mom sees Mr. Pygmy! If I was buying the hoglet for me, I would be worried, but she is not gonna say no to Pucci. Not on his birthday—not in front of Abuela Florita—and definitely not in front of Dad!

"Ain't you gonna get a cage, Chanel?" Aqua asks, concerned.

"Oh! I forgot about that," I say nervously. "Sir, do they poop in the cage?" Dorinda snickers.

"You can train them to use a litter box if you want," Mr. Magoo says.

Bubbles whips out her Miss Wiggy StarWac cell phone. "I'm calling Mom," she informs us. "Mom, can I borrow—wait a minute. Sir, how much is the cage?"

"Twenty-seven fifty," Mr. Magoo says.

"Mom, can I borrow twenty-seven fifty? We're still at the pet store, and we've gotta get Pucci a cage for the, um, hoggy. . . . Okay, *okay*."

Bubbles hands the phone to Mr. Magoo. "My mom is charging the cage." Then she turns to me, and says proudly, "The cage is on me. After all, I've gotta get Pucci something, too—since he did invite me to his party."

"How are you gonna pay for it?" I ask softly. Now I feel so guilty for fighting with Bubbles!

"Mom is holding the money I have left from our first gig, at the Kats and Kittys Club. Now I have nothing left."

I feel like crying, but I stammer, "I-I can't believe you had money left and you didn't tell me!"

"Why, Chuchie? So you could spend it?" Bubbles asks, laughing. Then she gives me a hug.

"Thank you, Bubbles. Pucci is gonna be so happy—because we are both his sisters."

We put Pucci's pet in his new cage. Then I hand Mr. Magoo the money for the hoglet. "I wonder if Mr. Pygmy can make noises, like 'Oink, oink!'" I say. I smile at Mr. Magoo, but he doesn't smile back at me.

"No, I don't think he can squeal like that," Bubbles says. Then she looks Mr. Magoo right in the face, and points her finger at him. "But I bet *this* one can!"

We hightail it out of that store, screaming with laughter, before Mr. Magoo fries *us* like *bacon*!

Chapter 11

It's a good thing I let Bubbles take Mr. Pygmy to her house, because the first "thing" I see when I open the door is nosy Pucci. The television is blaring from his bedroom, so I don't understand what my sneaky brother is doing in the foyer.

"Why are you out here?" I ask him.

"None of your business," he snips. Then he says, "I wonder what Daddy got me for my birthday," and runs back to his room, before I even have a chance to answer him.

I shake my head and laugh, because I realize that Pucci is probably so excited about his birthday tomorrow that he's already running to see who's at the door! I may have a sense of smell as keen as a dog's, but my brother has ears like a cat—he hears *everything*!

I debate whether I should tell Mom about the meeting at the record company, because I can hear that she is on the phone —probably talking to her boyfriend, Mr. Tycoon. He's probably in Paris, France—or anyway, in one of those places he lives.

Mom says he lives in Saudi Arabia, Paris, *and* Geneva, Switzerland. Places I've never been— but will get to see one day, now that I'm a Cheetah Girl. Bubbles says the Cheetah Girls are going to travel all over the world, until we're ready for the old cheetahs' retirement home.

I tiptoe into my bedroom and fall right into bed, hoping that I'll dream once again about the Benjamins falling from the sky. Or about all the fun the Cheetah Girls are going to have, recording songs with Mouse Almighty. . . .

The next morning, I'm s-o-o nice and helpful to Mom while we get everything ready for Pucci's birthday celebration. Humming along, I open the refrigerator and touch the bottles of *cerveza*—that's beer—to see if they're cold enough. My dad likes his *cerveza muy frío*—and we made sure to get his favorite, Wild Willy beer. I take out a few of the big brown bottles, and plunk them down on the banquet table.

"You seem very chirpy today, Chanel," Mom says, as she puts the big bowl of *fufu*—mashed yams—on the table.

"I'm happy it's Pucci's birthday," I say, all bubbly.

"Remember—don't say anything to your *abuela* about my boyfriend," Mom reminds me. "The last thing I need is for her blood pressure to go up because I'm not dating a Latin man."

"Okay, *Mamí*," I say, amused. I don't think Abuela *would* like Mom's boyfriend at all. He's *antipático*, if you ask me—not really friendly. But I guess I should just be grateful that any man would put up with Mom—because she can be a pain, *está bien?*

All of a sudden, I feel the "spookies" churning around in my stomach as a new thought occurs to me. *What if my father doesn't show up?*

No, he *has* to show up, I reassure myself. I hope Bubbles and *Madrina* don't get stuck in traffic either. I'd feel better if Bubbles was here.

Mom hands me the Dominican-style *arroz*

con pollo, and tells me to put it on the table. She puts the *sancocho* stew on the table herself, and tops it with slices of avocado. *Yum yum!*

"Pucci, you look cute!" I exclaim as he walks into the living room. He is wearing a red sweater and pants, his face is clean, and the curls on top of his head have been combed into place. I can tell he's really excited. Pucci sneaks over to the coffee table and starts rustling the wrapping paper on the big box that's sitting there.

"Cut it out, Pucci!" Mom yells from the kitchen. Pucci must get his keen sense of hearing from Mom, because she is the only person I know who has bigger ears than he does—*or* is more nosy!

When the doorbell rings, both Pucci and I run to answer it.

"I got it!" he hisses, so I stop short and let him open the door. It's his birthday.

"Hi, Pucci, darling!" *Madrina* says excitedly with outstretched arms. She grabs Pucci and gives him a big bear hug. Bubbles is right behind her, and she is holding a big cardboard box. I should have known these two would have a hideaway plan!

"What's that? Is it my present?" Pucci asks excitedly.

"Never mind, Mr. Cuckoo Cougar," Bubbles says jokingly, then puts down the box where it will be safely out of the way until it's time to open it.

"Bubbles, I have a joke for you!" Pucci says excitedly.

"Oh, I don't know, Pucci—your jokes aren't even fit for the ears of the wildest animals in the jiggy jungle," *Madrina* says hesitantly.

"Pucci!" Mom yells out.

"No, Auntie Dottie, this is a *good* one," Pucci says with a mischievous grin. Pucci calls *Madrina* "Auntie Dottie," even though she isn't really his aunt. (*Madrina* wanted to be Pucci's godmother as well as mine, but Dad let his sister, Aunt Lulu, be Pucci's godmother instead. Aunt Lulu lives in Miami, with three Chihuahuas—so of course, Mom never likes to visit her.)

"Okay, Pucci, let's hear the joke," Bubbles says, amused. I think she's trying to distract him from the box, 'cuz his eyes keep straying over in that direction.

"Okay. Why is it so hard to hide a cheetah like you?" he says.

"I don't know, Pucci . . . because I have a big mouth?" Bubbles responds.

"No! Because you're always *spotted*!" Pucci says proudly.

"Whew, that was a good one, Pucci, I must say," *Madrina* says, relieved. She sits down on the couch, takes off her big leopard hat, and hands it to me. *Madrina* hates it when her hat gets crushed, so I always put it in the closet until she leaves. That way, no one sits on it by mistake.

The doorbell rings again—but now I'm not worried about Pucci seeing his present, so I let him answer it.

"*Papí!*"

Gracias gooseness, my father is here! I close my eyes for a second, and ask God not to let my mom and dad fight today. Then I take a really deep breath and run to the door.

"Hi, Abuela!" I say loudly—because Abuela is hard-of-hearing. Abuela reaches up, with her walking cane in her hand, and gives me a hug.

I look up at my father and smile. He isn't really that tall, but next to my tiny *abuela*, he looks like a giant. Obviously, I take after Abuela, because I'm short, too.

Daddy hands Pucci a present, and I can tell Pucci is already sizing it up. My eyes are just as good as his, and from the shape of the present, I'd say it looks like a book.

I can't wait to tell my dad all about the Cheetah Girls' trip to Los Angeles, and big meeting with Def Duck Records! When we sit down, my dad's eyes are twinkling as I tell him *every* detail. Pucci squeezes in between him and Bubbles on the couch, and just looks on happily, listening.

"Who was that guy you were talking to after the showcase at the Tinkerbell Lounge, Chuchie?" Bubbles asks me, amused.

Why would Bubbles bring that up now—in front of my parents, no less?

"What guy?" I ask, playing innocent.

"The guy in the shiny suit and shades," Bubbles quips. "You remember . . ."

"Oh, that guy! He was a vice president for Def Duck—I think he said in the publicity department or something. I can't remember, Bubbles, *está bien?*"

"Well, I'll bet he remembers you, Miss

Chanel. As a matter of fact, everybody will, because they sure were giving you all the attention," Bubbles says, giggling.

Oh, I get it. Bubbles is trying to make me look important in front of Daddy!

"I don't think so, Bubbles—they were paying attention to *all* of us," I reply.

"What's this I hear about you flirting with some man, Chanel?" Mom yells from the dining room. "I hope you didn't go to Los Angeles and lose your mind!"

"No, *Mami*, I didn't," I say sheepishly.

Abuela is sitting across from me, and she just smiles. I don't think she really heard anything we said. *Gracias gooseness!*

"Juanita, you *knew* we were *all* working it," *Madrina* says, coming to my defense. "He *was* a tasty-looking morsel though, right, Chanel?"

What did *Madrina* have to say *that* for?!

All of a sudden, Mom snaps at *Madrina*, "If you're *that* hungry, Dottie, maybe you'd better eat something."

You can hear the *silencio.* Why does Mom have to pick on *Madrina* now? And why did *Madrina* have to start with her?

See, Mom and *Madrina* used to be models and

everything, and they were both really skinny. Mom is still skinny, because she never eats anything and exercises all the time. She is always picking on *Madrina* for getting, you know, *más grande.*

"Juanita, this isn't a restaurant, so rest assured I *will* serve myself—when everyone else eats," *Madrina* snips back at Mom, giving her that scary look that makes men run away on the street. *Por favor, Díos,* please—don't let *Madrina* hit Mom with her cheetah pocketbook!

Luckily, Dad comes to the rescue. "So—they gave you girls a record deal?"

"No, *Papí,* not exactly—well, I mean, no," I explain, stammering.

"Uncle Dodo, what Chanel means is, they're paying for us to record a few songs for a demo tape, then they'll see if they like the songs enough to give us a test single," Bubbles explains proudly. "And if *that* goes over well, *then* we get a record deal."

"Oh. I see."

Abuela beams at me, so I jump up and I run over to hug her. "Cristalle," she says, her eyes twinkling. Since last year, Abuela calls me by my confirmation name—which I like. *Me gusta Cristalle!*

"Let's eat!" I exclaim, jumping up to get everyone plates and stuff.

"Is there chicken in the *sancocho?*" Abuela asks Mom, while she spoons some onto her plate. The two of them are rival cooks—and the truth is, Abuela *does* cook better than Mom!

"No, I made it with just beef and pork this time," Mom says hesitantly.

"*Está bueno,*" Abuela says. Whew! Now we can all breath easier. If Abuela is happy with the food, then we're *all* happy!

I want to tell Dad that I saw Princess Pamela, but I realize he probably already knows that. Besides, Pucci is keeping him busy—he's so happy Dad is here.

After dinner, Mom goes to the kitchen, and motions for me to follow. That means it's time for Pucci's cake! We light the ten candles on top, and Mom brings it into the living room. I'm right behind her, singing, "Happy Birthday to you. Happy Birthday to you. Happy Birthday, dear Pucci . . . how old are you?"

We all join in and sing along, and Pucci finally blows out his candles. Now comes Pucci's favorite part: opening the presents! I'm glad, too, because I'm getting a new pet! Well,

Pucci's getting it—but I know who's gonna be taking care of it, and it's not gonna be Mom!

Pucci excitedly tears the wrapping paper off the box by the coffee table, opening his birthday present from Mom. "A new computer game— aren't you lucky!" I exclaim.

It's a great present, true—but I still can't believe she didn't get him a dog, after she promised she would. That's Mom for you.

"Mom, this is really cool!" Pucci says, giving her a big hug.

Mom looks at me over Pucci's shoulder, and I can tell she's thinking, "See? I didn't give him a dog and he's still happy, you troublemaker!"

Next, Pucci opens Abuela's present. It's a beautiful yellow and black sweater. She proudly tells him she knitted it herself, just for him.

"Thank you, Abuela," Pucci says, running over and hugging her.

Abuela urges Pucci to try it on, to make sure it fits. "My eyes aren't so reliable anymore, and you grow so fast," she says, smiling.

Pucci takes off his red sweater, and puts on his new one. "It fits!" he says proudly, warming Abuela's heart.

It's obvious that Pucci is saving Dad's present for last, because he opens *Madrina*'s next. *Madrina* has made Pucci a beautiful burgundy velvet suit.

"Oooh, Pucci, you are definitely the man!" Bubbles says excitedly.

"Thank you, Auntie Dottie," Pucci says, hugging *Madrina*.

"Make sure you wear that suit when you take your girlfriend out to a fancy restaurant." *Madrina* is always joking with Pucci about having a girlfriend. Pucci goes along with it, even though I know he *hates* girls—especially *me*.

"I will," he says, smiling and winking. He's so cute sometimes—even if he is a pain the rest of the time.

Bubbles goes and gets the cardboard carton, then sets it down in the middle of the floor. "Pucci," she says, "this present is from me and Chanel."

Pucci looks over at me and gives me a smile, even though I know he doesn't want to. Bubbles tries to help him open the box, but he insists on doing it himself.

"Oh, wow, what is it?" he exclaims excitedly, even though he doesn't know what kind of animal he's looking at. He pulls the cage out of the box carefully, and stares at Mr. Pygmy, completely transfixed.

"He's an African pygmy hedgehog," I say proudly, then look over at Mom to see if I should start packing and moving out yet.

She doesn't say a word, though.

"Wow, it looks like a—"

"Porcupine?" Bubbles asks, interrupting him.

"Yeah!"

Bubbles tells me with her eyes to take over.

"It's not a porcupine, because porcupines are rodents, Pucci. It's, um, related to moonrats," I explain.

"Wow, that's cool!" Pucci says, completely fascinated. He opens the cage door gingerly, and attempts to take Mr. Pygmy into his hands.

"Be careful," I warn. "He'll roll up into a ball and expose his spines when he's frightened."

"Oh, okay," Pucci says—but he doesn't seem to be afraid of Mr. Pygmy at all.

"He won't shed hair or anything so, um, you can't be allergic to them or anything," I say, looking at Mom with pleading eyes.

"Well, I hope you're gonna help him take

care of it—because I'm not going to," Mom huffs. Making a face, she gets up to get a Coke. That means she's upset, because she only drinks soda when she's upset. She would be afraid of the calories otherwise. As she pours the drink, she cuts her eyes sharply at me.

"What are you gonna name him, Pucci?" Bubbles asks.

"Cuckoo Cougar!" Pucci blurts out.

Cuckoo Cougar?! What a *stupid* name!!

"Oh, that's a nice name," Bubbles says, but I know she doesn't mean it. "We'll call him Cuckoo for short, okay?"

"Okay," Pucci says, smiling, as he puts Mr. Pygmy back in his cage.

Cuckoo. That's what *I'm* gonna call him anyway. Him *and* Pucci. Cuckoo one and cuckoo two!

At last, Pucci picks up the present Dad gave him, and rips off the paper. It *is* a book—and from the look on Pucci's face, I realize it's a book that *he* doesn't *like*.

Pucci holds the book in his hand and stares at the cover, then throws it on the floor! "I don't want this!" he says, pouting.

I can't believe Pucci! I run over and pick up the book, and look at the cover. It says, *Harry Henpecker's Guide to Geography.*

What was Dad thinking? This is the kind of *boring* book they always make us read in school!

Pucci runs over to Abuela and puts his head on her shoulder. He really is a big crybaby. *How could he hurt Dad's feelings like that?*

But I already know the answer. Pucci is very angry at Dad for leaving us. Poor Pucci—he doesn't realize that it has nothing to do with him. He doesn't care that Dad and Mom don't love each other anymore—he just wants Dad to live with us again.

I get up from the floor and go to sit by Dad. He doesn't say anything for a long time. Then, very calmly, he says, "You said that Pucci doesn't read anything, and I was just trying to help."

"I understand, Dodo," Mom says, looking embarrassed. I can tell she wants to yell at Pucci, but she feels bad for him because it's his birthday.

"Pucci," Mom says sternly, looking at my brother. "*Papí* is going to get you another birthday present, okay?"

"*Don't* tell him that!" Dad blurts out. I can tell he is getting *caliente* mad, because his eyes are getting red, and he's breathing fire.

"Okay, I'm sorry," Mom says. "But it wouldn't hurt you to get him something else."

I can't believe how nice she's being! I'm so glad it's Pucci's birthday—otherwise, they'd be throwing pots and pans at each other by now!

"If he weren't so spoiled, he would appreciate any present that he got. I didn't get any presents at all when I was a child," Dad says sternly. See, he and Auntie Lulu were secretly smuggled out of Cuba when they were kids. After that, they never saw their father again. I can tell it still hurts Dad.

He gets up very slowly, and tells Abuela that it's time to go. Mom doesn't say a word while they get their coats.

"I love you, *Papí*," I whisper in his ear, then kiss him good-bye. He hugs me tight. I hug Abuela tight, too—she's so very precious to me.

"*Gracias Dios*," Mom says when Dad and Abuela are gone. Shaking her head, she gets up and goes into the den.

Mom *never* talks in Spanish, so I know she

must be very upset. She probably is going to call Mr. Tycoon now, and talk for hours and hours.

Pucci wipes away his tears, then goes over to the cage and picks up Mr. Pygmy. "Chanel, I like your and Bubbles's present the best." Then, quickly, he turns to *Madrina* and adds, "Yours, too, Auntie Dottie!"

"I know, darling—don't think I feel bad," *Madrina* says, picking up her glass of soda. "I can't blame you, Pucci. Nobody wants to read schoolbooks on their birthday! You'd·think we could just forget about that drama for at least one day!"

I smile at Bubbles. She turns to Pucci and says, "Next time someone gives you a present you don't like, you shouldn't hurt their feelings, Pucci."

"Okay," Pucci says. I guess he feels bad now for acting like a spoiled brat.

"Just pretend you like it. Then, later, you can toss it in the giveaway pile in the closet and recycle it!" *Madrina* says.

Bubbles and I look at each other and laugh— because once, *Madrina* forgot that Mom gave her a navy blue scarf for Christmas, and she gave it back to Mom the next year. Her "recycling rodeo" backfired!

I hug Pucci. I know how much it hurts to be disappointed—especially now that I'm part of the Cheetah Girls, and our lives have turned into a roller-coaster ride. One day, we're up and flying high, the next day we're screaming our heads off as we descend to the bottom.

"You're not such a bad sister after all," Pucci says, cracking a smile for the first time since Dad left.

"You wanna come and see my room?" I ask him. I *never* let Pucci come into my room, because he is so nosy.

"Okay," he says, and I can tell he's happy I asked him.

Bubbles follows us. "I'm gonna stay over," she says, hugging me.

"Great!" Pucci says, because he really does love Bubbles —I think even more than he loves me.

Pucci, Mr. Pygmy, Bubbles, and I all lie on the bed together.

"Are you really gonna make songs together?" Pucci asks me. Mr. Pygmy's little body is cupped in his right hand, and Pucci is tickling him.

"Yeah, Pucci, we *are* gonna make songs together," I say, without looking up at him. "Bubbles, can you believe we're getting a chance to record songs for a real record label?"

There is silence for a second; then Bubbles blurts out, "Yeah, I can't believe it! I just pray to God that they don't have us recording songs like the ones Pumpmaster Pooch made us do."

I wince at the memory of the producer we worked with for a Minute Rice moment. Mr. Jackal Johnson, our former manager, teamed us with Pumpmaster Pooch and put us in a studio. We recorded songs that made us sound like a pack of gangsta hyenas!

"*Gracias gooseness*, *Madrina* got us out of that one," I say, sighing. "What was the name of that song we recorded for them? It was *horrible*."

"'I Got a Thing for Thugs,'" Bubbles says, without missing a beat. "If Def Duck Records makes us record songs as wack as that, Chuchie, the Cheetah Girls are gonna rent a hot-air balloon—and head off to OZ!"

Giggling, I lay my head on Bubbles's shoulder and say, "You always said we were gonna follow the yellow brick road, no matter where it leads."

All of a sudden, I remember the dream I had—the one with me and Bubbles flying with an umbrella. And I also remember Princess Pamela's prediction—that good things were gonna start happening. "I don't think we're gonna need that hot-air balloon, Bubbles," I tell her.

"Why?" Bubbles asks.

"'Cuz I just heard a weather report in my head—*it's gonna be raining Benjamins!*"

It's Raining Benjamins

For the first time in her-story
*there's a weather forecast
that looks like the mighty cash.
So tie up your shoes and
put away your blues
'cuz we're going around the bend
at half past ten
to the only place in town
where everything is coming up green
you know what I mean:*

*It's raining Benjamins
for a change and some coins
It's raining Benjamins
I heard that
It's raining . . . again!*

*Now maybe you're wondering
what's all the thundering—
but we've got the root of all the loot
that got past Santa's chute
without collecting soot.*

So put on your galoshes
and bring your noshes
to the only place in town
where money is falling on the ground.
That's right, y'all:

It's raining Benjamins
for a change and some coins
It's raining Benjamins
I heard that
It's raining . . . again!

So here's the rest of the her-story
Now that there's no longer a mystery.
There's precipitation in the nation
and it's causing a sensation
in the only way that dollar bills
can give you thrills.
Yeah, that's what I mean:

It's raining Benjamins
for a change and some coins
It's raining Benjamins
I heard that
It's R-A-I-N-I-N-G . . . AGAIN!
(Say it, again!)

The Cheetah Girls Glossary

Adobo down: Mad flava.

Antipático: Dodo. Lame. Pain in the poot-butt.

Babosa: Stupid.

Bacalao: Spanish codfish.

Beeneh: Romanian for "good."

Benjamins: Bucks, dollars.

Bobada: Baloney.

Bugaboo: Pain in the butt.

Cerveza: Beer.

El pollito: Acting like a chicken.

Está bien: Okay, get it?

Gnocco: Italian for "blockhead."

Goospitating: Nervous.

Gracias gooseness: Thank goodness!

I'm so over this: Fed up to the max.

La dopa: Dope-licious.

La gente: Peeps, people.

Lonchando: Spanglish for lunch.

Madrina: Godmother.

Madrino: Godfather.

Montagna: Mountain—or a diamond ring as big as one!

Off the cheetah meter: Beyond cheetah-licious. Off the hook. Supa-dupa chili.

Pata de puerco: Idiot. Leg of a pig.

Poot-butt: Someone who is a pain or has a funny-looking booty.

Que puzza!: Italian for "what a stinky-poo."

The spookies: A nightmare. The willies.

Un coco: A crush.

Vampira: A vampire.

Wait for the bait: Wait for the right moment to pounce on an "op"—an opportunity.